THE LEGEND OF THE SWAN HORSE

Charlie + Cathy,
God bless you
and your family
with love, laughter
+ joy!
God Bless!
Darby Lynn Gaynor
Jeremiah 29:11

THE LEGEND OF THE SWAN HORSE

DARBY LYNN GAYNOR

Pleasant Word
A Division of WINEPRESS PUBLISHING

Printed in the United States of America

Packaged by Pleasant Word, a division of WinePress Publishing, PO Box 428, Enumclaw, WA 98022. The views expressed or implied in this work do not necessarily reflect those of Pleasant Word, a division of WinePress Publishing. Ultimate design, content, and editorial accuracy of this work are the responsibilities of the author.

ISBN 1-4141-0162-7
Library of Congress Catalog Card Number: 2004103842

Table of Contents

Acknowledgments

There are so many who have helped and encouraged me in the writing of this book. I wish to thank the many proofreaders that diligently persevered in reading, correcting errors, and giving valuable insights while the story was still in rough form. They were: Hannah Dennis, Nathan Dennis, Kathy Dufault, Kevin Dye, Chandra Flores, Debbie Howell, Craig Phillips, Jessie, Sheila Pribble, Charlie Ross, Rachel Ross, Lois Saget, Barbara Taylor-Brett, and Don and Marge Timmons. Ginny Scorup has my eternal gratitude for her computer expertise.

My special thanks go to my two children, Nathan and Hannah, for their encouragement and love over the years. Not only did they proofread the book, but endured many hardships as this story was being written in my life.

Most of all I want to give thanks to God for His great mercy, patience, love, and forgiveness. Without Him I would have no hope. He is my strength. He is my joy. He is my salvation! I thank him for taking my broken life and dreams and working it out for good.

Chapter One

Daniel and Sara felt the magic of the night disappearing. The pleasant frog and cricket symphony they had been listening to under the velvety jewel laden canopy of nightfall transitioned to a sickening cacophony as they drew closer to the project housing. At last they reached their own building. They ascended the stairs and fled past the gauntlet of soul shredding verbosities to the haven behind their own door. Abusive, people-hating chants and resounding booms shook the whole living zone like a giant pulsing hate alarm.

"Mom, my stomach hurts. It doesn't feel much like Christmas anymore. I wish Dad were here. He always made me feel safe and happy." Sara looked sadly at her sensitive son. She too felt the heaviness of the chaos and misery around her. Her mind wandered to the magical book in her grandmother's old wooden chest that was said to contain the mysteries of life. What had grandmother said? Something about the danger of reading it . . . because it was alive.

She found herself walking to the trunk at the foot of her bed. Her great grandmother's favorite stuffed toy, a wonderful old goat, was sticking out of the box. Great grandfather's favorite stick horse was wedged into the opening. Off to the side, half exposed, was the book she sought. She stared at its ornate cover and the winged horses and dragons that graced it.

Daniel silently slid to his mother's side. Softly he whispered, "Mom. That's the book I want us to read."

"It is a very old and magical story, Son. I don't know if we should read it, Sweetheart. My grandmother warned that the story would change your life forever."

"Mom, I want us to read that story. It wants us to read it."

Sara glanced quizzically at her son. Did he, too, feel drawn to this book? She studied his face for a clue. Much to her surprise he answered her question. "Mom, we have to read it. I feel it in my heart. Please. It's all right. I'm not afraid."

"All right, Son, you go get the Christmas candle and light it, and I'll fix the hot chocolate." They both scurried off to their tasks. It had become a Christmas Eve tradition to light a candle in memory of loved ones that couldn't be with them and to read a book by its light, while drinking hot chocolate. It helped them feel less alone in the world.

Carefully, Daniel lit the candle and whispered, "God, please say *Hi* to Dad and tell him I love him." He glanced around to make sure his mom wasn't near. "And, could you tell him I'm worked hard and earned enough money to get Mom a nice warm coat at the Salvation Army Store. It's her Christmas surprise."

Sara carried in two cups of hot chocolate and then went to get the book. It was very old and rather large. The pages were rustling as though whispering to her.

They sipped some of the steaming chocolate and snuggled up together. Sara held the book on her lap. Magic hung in the air. She and Daniel both shivered involuntarily with excitement.

Sara slowly opened the book. A hush hung heavy in the air. The very first entry was a beautiful handwritten note which Sara softly read.

"Have you ever had a vision so beautiful and so real that you felt as if you'd been given a great gift? I had such a vision once during a very hard time in my life. In the dream I was a white horse running along the ocean's edge in the moonlight. Flying next to me was a glorious white swan. As we traveled along the shimmering waters edge, the swan began to merge with me until all you could see were his wings! Suddenly I was airborne and flying among the stars. I felt so free and joyful. For years I wondered at the meaning of the dream, and God revealed to me the story He had written in my life.

"The story is not just for me, but for everyone in need of hope or needing to know that someone cares. I have treasured and pondered it for these past months and kept it guarded closely in my heart. Lately there has come an urgency to set it free. Deep in my heart I know now it was not just for me. It belongs to many others and longs to touch their hearts and change their lives as it has mine.

"The dream is full of hidden mysteries. See it with the eyes of your spirit; listen from the depths of your heart that you may truly know what I have come to know. Its truths have become a fire within me, burning fiercely, yet not destroying me . . . only melting off the chains that have bound me these many years. I am set free! I can fly! If you are faint hearted, stop now, for the dream *will* pass to you. It starts as a spark and grows till it is a raging fire within. You will see yourself by the light of the fire as you have never seen yourself before.

"Once having truly seen yourself, you will have a choice to make. Depending on your choice the fire will either burn away your chains and set you free or totally destroy you. That is your choice. And now . . . I shall share with you my dream."

Sara and Daniel snuggled closer. Reassuringly, she hugged his shoulders. Softly he touched her hand and looked at her with somber gaze. "I'm not afraid Mom. Let's read the story."

"Yes, in my heart I know I won't rest till I know its secrets. You know it's almost as though someone who loved me was calling my name. I do wish your father were here." Lovingly she gazed at the picture of her handsome husband. The pale blue Christmas candle shone brightly beside it.

"Mom, Dad knows about the book. When he was sick I saw him reading it. He said I was too little to understand but one day, when the time was right, I should read it." A tear rolled down Sara's cheek as she gazed intently at her husband's picture. Tears were flowing freely now in twin streams down her cheeks.

Daniel took her hands in his own small ones and looked lovingly in his mother's eyes. "Mom, the day Dad died he pulled me into his arms and whispered in my ear, 'Tell your mom to be sure to read this book. Tell her I'll see her again, and I love her.'" He dropped his head and lowered his eyes in pain. "That's when he went to sleep and didn't wake up." Great drops of liquid emotion splashed to his hands.

"Mom, I'm sorry. I forgot to tell you." His young body shook convulsively with the greatness of the pain it tried so valiantly to contain, but to no avail. The more he tried to hold it back the stronger it crashed within his tender heart until finally it broke through in a raging torrent of tears.

When the flood subsided and he regained control, haltingly, between gulps of cleansing air, he spoke, "It didn't make a lot of sense to me. I forgot what he told me till you read the first part. All of a sudden I remembered his words." Painfully, he lifted his tear-stained face to search her eyes for the comfort he now so desperately needed. He was not disappointed.

Sara pulled her young son close to her heart as the pain of lost love ripped it open. It was the boy in her arms that drew her focus back to the present and the precious gift her husband had left. Here in her arms was a part of him. She was not alone. It was comforting to know that whatever this story was about, he had approved of their reading it.

Somehow it seemed less threatening, almost comforting, for now she and her son would retrace at least part of his steps from his last days on earth. With soft sighs of relief, they hugged, snuggled closer and settled down for the story. The storm had washed away a bit of their hidden pain. A peaceful quiet settled in their hearts. Softly Sara began to read.

Chapter Two

It was a time of despair and deep sadness. A thick darkness smothered the land. The cheery light and warmth of the sun was only spoken of in ancient legends. No-one was sure if a sun even existed, or what it really was. After all, they had never seen it. Perhaps it was only a legend of the Old Ones. Only the harsh glaring neon lights of the local taverns, gambling halls, and bordellos cut into the constant gloomy gray of the day and thick black of the night.

The signs flashed enticingly with promises of a "Happy Hour," or "Instant Riches," and "Lovemaking at its Finest." Those going into the taverns did not come out happy, only staggering and incoherent. Often they were angry and combative. Sometimes it seemed as if they were sleep walking, oblivious to their surroundings. Some stumbled and fell and slept where they lay. Others actually made it home. Most were not greeted joyously by their families. Many families hid because of the ugly mood the drink would put their loved one in. Many a family member had learned the hard way that it was best to stay out of the way of one "under the influence." No, no happiness was here. Some referred to the drink as *spirits*, but they were not happy spirits.

Those that came out of the gambling halls seldom came out wealthy. Most lost what little they had. Some lost everything, even their homes, and had to roam the streets. The promised love seemed to give only disease, a sense of emptiness, and a true feeling of loneliness. Most who sold their bodies actually lost what chance they had at real love. They felt used and cheap. They had sold their bodies for drugs or money or pure instant pleasures. When they were used up, they were tossed aside for someone younger and more beautiful or more handsome, for both sexes were on the market peddling their bodies. The old were sad, lonely individuals, no loving companion, no joyous memories, no hope for the future. Everyone dreaded growing old, lest they be discarded as rubbish.

All who were able were required to work in order to earn money to pay for a place to stay and food to eat. The jobs didn't pay well and required most to be away from their little ones to earn enough for everyone to eat. The taskmasters owned the neon houses and encouraged the workers to go and forget their troubles after work. The sad creatures didn't enjoy their jobs or spend time with their families but lived for the weekends and the neon houses. After all, the story boxes declared that if you partied, then you were living life to the fullest.

At home, the children were provided with picture boxes to help ward off the loneliness. The taskmasters owned the story stations and made sure the stories would prepare the little ones for a life of working for them. The neon houses were portrayed as life's ultimate pleasure, and acquiring the things the taskmasters made were portrayed as life's main goal.

I saw the rowdiness and emptiness of the night. I saw families in meadows and dusty corrals, fancy stables and plain old barns. This was not a land inhabited by people but by horses and dragons. Many a tear and silent, sickening cry was uttered in the night. There was no joy. There was no hope. All was dismal and drudgery. A heavy darkness had swallowed the land and its inhabitants.

When the gray of morning finally came, I saw a young colt wiping away the tears of the night. Her mother nuzzled her gently and began biting and pulling at the restrictive collar on her little one's neck. She wore a collar herself. Everyone did. All inhabitants wore these tracking devices. This was how the overlords maintained control.

Solemnly the mother spoke, "I must go to work again today." She wearily sighed. "This dusty corral is no place for a little one." Finally with one last wrenching bite, the collar was torn off. "Go, Child. Go look and see if there is truly a place where a sun shines and waters run clear, where grasses and flowers are so lush and deep that one need ever go hungry. I don't wish for you to live as I have had to. It shrivels your spirit till you are weary and hopeless. There is nothing good to look forward to. Go, Child. Run fast and far. And . . ." she faltered, her voice full of emotion as she looked to some far off place of long ago, "if you should find such a place, grow strong and when you can, return to me and tell me what you find. My heart longs to go with you, but I am too weary for the journey."

"A long time ago, my great grandmother told me of such a place where horses ran wild and free . . . and they could fly," she whispered wistfully. "They were their own masters and served a great Father, a Father of Lights. Oh, Little One, I shall miss you. You will be in danger, but I would rather you die trying to find something better. To live here is certain death and it is, oh, so slow. You must take care, for the servants of the Darklord will be searching for you. You must not be found; you must escape!"

As her little one left and vanished into the gloomy mists, she wept bitterly. She would miss this little one, but wanted her to have a chance at something better. "Oh Father of Lights, if you are indeed real, please watch over my little messenger I have sent to find you. Guide her path, grant her a life of freedom and beauty, and send her back to us with a message from you. Protect her from the Darklord."

Sadly she turned and carried the detested little collar out to the field and stomped the tracking device to bits. Then she dropped the remains into a gopher hole. Perhaps they could make something useful out of it. At least it would be hidden from view of the Darklord's spies.

Meanwhile, the little colt slowly and quietly picked her way through the gray mists. When she would hear nearby hooves or dragon feet she would freeze and let the mists hide her. Occasionally, she would hear another youngster nearby quietly sobbing in loneliness. Some youngsters bickered and others sat spellbound in front of the story boxes. All the little ones were alone. (That was what the Darklord wanted.) Soon she came to the fields where the parents labored. Some pulled plows, others hauled carts of wood and stone, or food. Quite a few of the adults were required to go deep into the caves of the earth and bring out precious darkstones or twinkle rocks. Some died when the earth decided to chomp down and close a hole. That didn't stop the Darklord. He just had others make new holes.

It was a very hard thing to go in search of something new. What if she didn't find it? What if the Darklord's servants captured her on the way? Even though life at home was miserable, she had grown used to it. It was comfortable in its own weird way. At least there she knew what to expect. This did not feel good. In fact, it was downright scary.

The little colt ambled along, lost in her disturbing thoughts. Suddenly, a bright flash jolted her to attention. It was a neon house. She'd seen them on the story box. The hot pink sign flashed and buzzed in an irritating way. Some of the "fancy" mares and "dandy" dragons beckoned to her. The fanciest old mare called out, "Come here, Little One, we will make a beauty out of you. Everyone will want you."

As she looked at them, it seemed they were all paint and feathers. They didn't look as beautiful as her mother. She felt a questioning knot in her stomach. Something here did not feel right, and she galloped quickly away. The place had a bad feel to it, as though it wanted to eat her alive! As soon as she was far enough away she shuddered, trying to rid herself of the awful feeling.

Up ahead was another neon house. Cautiously, she approached. A silky voice called out to her, "Come, Child. I will give you sweet wine. You'll forget your troubles. Come join the party."

She looked hard at the owners. They didn't look like they really cared about her troubles. The party animals didn't look happy. They seemed pitiful and did foolish things. No, this place did not feel good either. It felt like a place she might get lost in and never find her way out!

Again she ran, but straight up to the gilded doors of yet another neon house! Lights were flashing frantically. The whole place was lit up in a blazing display. "Come take a chance, make a fortune in minutes! It only takes a quarter!" called the door attendant excitedly.

She looked hard at the owner. He didn't really want to make her rich, or he'd just give her the money. No, she felt like he was a trickster. He only wanted to take away what she had, not give her what he had. Quickly she galloped off. The place felt like a vacuum that wanted to suck away all she owned.

"Finally I have escaped the neon houses! This all feels so bad," she spoke aloud to herself. "Maybe I should just go back." Quietly on the bank of the Murky River, she cried. This was really hard! Up ahead she saw the place of towers. Over her left shoulder she saw a large stadium with brightly colored flags. Several beautiful horses were being lead in through a gate. Her heart quickened. Maybe the flying horses were here! This might be a good place to check. As she trotted over, the beautiful horses turned up their noses at her. "You are obviously not one of us! We have ribbons in our lovely manes and gorgeous silk blankets on our backs.

We stay in the fanciest of stables—no place for the likes of you! We are strong and swift and beautiful."

Embarrassed and ashamed, she backed away, stumbling awkwardly as she tried to make herself disappear. How could she have possibly thought she might fit in with the truly beautiful horses? From a distance she gazed longingly at them. Then she noticed they were tied off. Soon some funny little monkeys dressed in fancy silk outfits came and made them run in a giant circle as fast as they could. The winner got some weird flowers hung around its neck and the monkey got some money.

"Hmmm, I wonder where the old horses are."

During the race she had noticed that one of the older horses just couldn't keep up. As if in answer to her question, a giant cart pulled up and loaded the older slower horse onto it. It was headed back down the road she had just traveled.

Well, these horses obviously weren't wild and free. Maybe they didn't have it as good as they thought they did. Slowly, she turned her head towards the city. She would follow the road like her mother had asked her to.

Night was falling. It wasn't a definite sort of thing; everything was already gray. It just got darker till finally it was impenetrable. She ran quickly to the Murky River for a drink and then munched some of the scruffy grasses. There was a bridge nearby. It would be a good place to hide for the night. Tiredly, she drug her little feet. Rest was desperately needed.

Suddenly, she snapped to attention, almost jumping out of her skin. A soft little snort had come from the shadows. Every muscle was rigid. Turning towards the sound she braced herself for the worst. "Who's there?" her voice quavered.

Out of the darkness pounced a handsome young horse still wearing his tracking collar. He noticed hers was gone. "Hey, where's your collar?" he demanded.

Frightened at his question, she began backing away in preparation to flee.

"I'm not going to hurt you," he said more gently. He really didn't want to frighten her. "I just wondered how you got yours off. I wish I could get rid of mine. Then I could really go places. Right now I can only get away for a little bit and then they drag me back."

"Maybe I could chew it off for you," she offered.

"These collars are pretty tough. I doubt your teeth could chew through before they find me. Then they might really get mad and wonder if someone were nearby helping me. No," he said, looking at her tenderly and noticing for the first time that she was kind of cute in her own way. He cocked his head to the side and smiled a winning grin. "I can't have them taking a pretty girl like you back to the stables. They'll be here soon. When they come, I'll jump out and run. You stay way back in the shadows. Without your tracking collar they won't find you."

Shyly, she lowered her head and looked at him through her lashes. He was very handsome and noble. Her heart raced unexplainably at the sight of him. "You are very brave to protect me that way."

"Aw, it's nothing." But as he spoke, a smile rose to his lips. Now he was looking directly into her eyes. Magic was in the air. A soft warm glow encircled the two of them.

"Where are you going?" he asked softly, not wanting to break the spell of the moment, but wanting to know where to find her.

"I'm going in search of deep grasses, clear water, and to see if I can find the horses that fly."

"I wish I could go with you," he said longingly. "Hey, we'd better get back in the shadows before they find us both." He led her back to his favorite hiding place. Gratefully she followed, wondering at the strange feeling he had awakened in her. She'd never felt so toasty and weak and wonderful like this before. She longed to brush up against him to feel his warmth. As if in answer to her thoughts, he nuzzled her. Softly, he whispered in her ear. "I will never forget you. Never forget me. If you find the flying horses come and tell me about them. How I would love to fly!"

She nuzzled his neck and listened to the steady beat of his heart. Oh how she wanted to stay with this brave friend forever. Even in the shadows she could see the strength and sincerity in his eyes. They were bright with intelligence and full of courage and daring. She knew that she would be able to depend on him.

Suddenly, there was the sound of dragons' feet thudding as they landed. Their great leathery wings fanned the air to break their fall. The Darklord had given those who would follow him some hideous leathery wings. It was the mark of their loyalty to him. Even some of the horses had become his servants and were given the same disgusting bone and leather wings. Yes, they could fly, but her mother had told her that these were not the wings spoken of in days of old.

The wings of freedom were different from the wings of bondage. Her mother had told her that the bondage wings were only a poor attempt to mimic the real and everlasting wings of the Father. The Darklord's wings often fall apart, crashing the wearer to their death. Though they flew for awhile and felt important they were really after all only slaves to one who didn't care if they were destroyed or not. Yes, she knew that these were not the horses she sought.

Her friend kissed her neck ever so softly and whispered in her ear, "Be careful; don't forget me," and with that final word, he bounded out of the shadows and led them on a merry chase. Finally, they captured him and escorted him back to his cave and chained him to the wall for the night. The cave did not seem quite so gloomy somehow, for in his heart he carried his new friend. His thoughts drifted off to her and her journey. He hoped she would be safe. How he wished he could join her, perhaps one day.

Meanwhile, the young colt shivered in the night still hidden under the bridge. She wondered what had happened to her brave new friend. Thoughts of him warmed her and helped dispel the sense of loneliness that was trying to overcome her. Black was turning to gray; it was time to be on her way. She sucked in deeply trying to gather the courage to cross the bridge and pass through the city.

Somehow she managed to force her feet to take her into the city. Vendors everywhere tried to get her to work for them in return for a corral to stay in and hay at the end of the day. Her heart told her that she would only end up like her mother if she did this. But, for a little while she pulled a wagon in return for a safe place to sleep and food to eat. She was a bit frightened about what might lie beyond the city. One day, though, she'd had enough and left. Her heart had grown restless. She knew she must continue her journey. The city seemed a place of resignation and constant meaningless activity that never really changed anything. This place felt like a giant trap.

It was good to be on the road again, a little frightening but good. Somewhere deep within, her feelings were stirring again. She felt excitement at what might lie ahead. After all, she was still alive and had passed through many things unharmed. This wasn't so bad. The road finally took her out of the city. The lights glaring in the haze behind her began to fade. Now the road became steeper and seemed to disappear before her. What if it came to an end, then what?

Something dark was up ahead. She couldn't quite make it out. As she got closer she realized that what she was seeing were lots and lots of trees growing side by side. This must be the forest some of the grownups had talked about from time to time. She'd heard tales of wolves and panthers and bears that could and would eat her! Oh, what to do, what to do!

She had passed fields, neon houses and a city. She had escaped them all, but this she knew nothing about. It was hard to face the things she feared. She could go back and live like her mother. That at least would be familiar. Why was she on this journey anyway? She'd seen so much and was so weary. Rest was her main thought. Finally, she decided to only go a little way into the forest. She could run out if it became too scary.

The giant trees whispered gently in the breeze. The darkness became thicker. Rustling noises of soft feet made the hair stand up on her back. Still, she resolutely proceeded. At last she bedded down, cold and exhausted.

Morning came with a flurry of activity. Forest creatures scurried about busily eating and playing and checking her out. This place wasn't so frightening. It actually felt good. It felt friendly . . . like it was glad she was there. She ate hungrily of the soft green grasses. Suddenly she stood absolutely petrified. Bright rays of light pierced through the trees and totally bathed her in their glowing warmth.

At first she was frightened, though not for long. It felt so good. The warmth seemed to reach all the way to her insides. *Oooooo* . . . this was lovely. The peace of the moment, the beauty of her surroundings, and the pleasure of the warmth overcame her and she wept. She wished her mom were with her now. The stories were true; there was a peaceful place with grass and clear water and sunshine!

Soon the light was gone, but now she remembered why she had come. Her courage had returned, her strength was renewed, and there was something new inside of her. For the first time in her life she had hope of a new and better tomorrow.

Slowly, she continued the climb. Beads of sweat rose from her body and mingled with the dust of the trail. Her muscles began to ache in weariness. The path grew steeper. Often she would stumble, or find herself slipping backwards on the loose gravel. Heavy branches tore at her as she crashed wearily through the sometimes-overgrown trail. Her knees had become a mass of oozing cuts. Her heart was steadfast, though. She must see what was at the end of this road. It wasn't traveled much, but she could tell it had been used, though not recently. Secretly she began to hope that perhaps she might see the flying horses. Perhaps they were not just a legend after all!

Strangely, even though the way had become treacherous, she felt a deep sense of peace. She knew in her heart that she was doing what she should be doing. Stranger still, she realized she didn't feel lonely. It was almost as if something or someone was drawing her on this journey. She remembered the distant look in her mother's eye. Had she attempted the journey long ago? She must ask her when she saw her again.

Many puzzling thoughts were flowing through her mind. Who owned this place? Why was no one else here? Who took care of all the animal friends? Where did that bright light come from? Why didn't mom come with me? Could I stay here forever? I own nothing really; here I have everything I need. Somehow, up here, working for a stable to live in and a corral plus hay and oats seemed silly. It even seemed silly to be one of the fancy racehorses with all of their riches.

Resolutely she plodded on. The clouds were thinning, and the air seemed sweeter. Then abruptly she reached the top. There was a very steep and narrow trail dropping into white mists below. The way looked treacherous. As she scanned the mists her eyes suddenly grew large in awe at the sight before her. To the right she saw golden mesas bathed in light with blue rivers cutting through the land. What a glorious place!

Her heart froze in wonder as she saw horses racing and playing. They looked so . . . so free. To her great amazement, one of the horses jumped across a large gorge. Could it be? Was it possible? Were these flying horses? Oh, how her heart ached to know. Tears ran down her tired, dirty face. If only it were true! The creatures vanished into the mesas and she could not quite make out if they had wings or not.

Her eyes continued to follow the skyline to the left. Mesas melted into gentle green rolling hills with scattered patches of blue water and occasional rivers. Those dots . . . were they possibly more horses? It looked *soooo* peaceful—all the grass and water one could possibly want! The hills rose higher and higher till they came to the edge of the most beautiful purple mountains. They were bathed in lovely violet light.

Something was moving on the pinnacle of one of the craggy peaks. She squinted, trying desperately to make out what it was. Her heart quivered with excitement as she saw a horse raise two glorious wings and fly from the peak, dipping and circling effortlessly on the mountain breezes. Spellbound she watched till all she could see was a tiny speck. She stood transfixed for hours, taking in all she had seen, realizing that there was a life different from what she had known. Could she go there? Would they let her stay even though she was just an ordinary little horse with no wings? As the last rays of the sun bathed her in their crimson, violet rays she knew in her heart that somehow, some way she must find the winged horse. Out loud to no one in particular she wishfully spoke. "I wish I knew about the flying horses. I wish I knew how to get to them."

As night fell she slept an exhausted sleep. Troubling dreams of her past flashed through her mind. Pictures of the journey she had taken, all of the neon houses and riches were beckoning to her. There was the strong silent pull to be with the wild flying horses and always the treacherous trail going into the mist. Did she dare attempt the journey?

Chapter Three

The young colt was awakened by the sound of hooves striking heavily on stone and a lot of huffing and puffing. Something huge was coming her way! Terrified, she darted quickly behind some young saplings and trembled as quietly as she could, barely breathing at all. Suddenly, a huge ram with massive horns arose from the moonlit mists; the night had not yet passed. She almost fainted from fright. Should she run or face him? Moonbeams glittered in his eyes and danced on his white furry face. The winds tugged gently at his rich, silvery white hair. There was a gentleness about him, a kindness in his eyes. Actually, he looked very wise. Then he spoke, "Child, do not fear me, I have come in answer to your wishes."

"My wishes?" she stammered. Oh boy, was she in trouble now! Desperately, she tried to remember having ever wished to see such a creature. No, there were no clues. How could she have possibly wished him when she didn't even know what he was!

As if in answer to her frantic thoughts he spoke again, softly and soothingly, "Did you wish to know of those that fly?"

Ah, that wish. "Yes . . ." she spoke hesitantly, yet eagerly.

"I have come to tell you their story and to show you the way if you care to go."

Her curiosity and desire to know of the flying ones burned strong within her. Consciously she chose to trust the creature and nodded her assent to his questioning eyes.

"I shall sing of the ancient magic. You must listen with all your heart." Softly, the great creature began to sing the ancient words. How gently they fell on her ears and stirred her heart to life. She felt its magical weavings until she no longer saw him at all, only the legend sprung to life on the moonlit mists before them, and on he sang.

As she watched spellbound she beheld the Great One, The Father of Lights in radiant splendor. His robe sparkled with shimmering lights of many colors. He was both fearsome and gentle all at once. As she gazed upon Him, she scarcely noticed the surroundings, for He was so magnificent! She found herself casting her eyes down in humility. Here was greatness such as she had never known. There was strength, truth, and love in His eyes. A great feeling of unworthiness engulfed her, and yet a resounding joy was rising within. Here was someone who could see to the very depths of her soul. Involuntarily, she cringed lest His piercing gaze fall on her, for surely it would consume her, and yet . . . she longed to rush to His arms and weep for joy.

Out of the corner of her eye she caught a glimpse of a multitude of beings. Some were hairless creatures in tunics. There were several animals, many of which she'd never seen before. Some were creatures beyond her scope of knowledge. Different though they were, all had a simple honest look about them. They seemed clean and lovely, though all were not what you would call beautiful. She noticed a softness behind each one. At first, she thought it was a light of some sort, for glints of color like the fire of the twinkle rocks would catch her eye. Then one of the creatures moved, and she realized that what she was seeing was a beautiful, iridescent pair of feathery wings. She marveled at all the lovely winged creatures. She felt as if she'd known them all her life and that she could tell them anything and they'd love her anyway. She trusted them. In their eyes she saw truth and compassion. It was obvious they loved the Great Father by the adoration in their eyes. They seemed also to care for each other.

Off to one side, she noted some handsome but haughty creatures. They kept sneaking looks at each other out of the corners of their eyes to see if anyone was noticing their beauty; there was also distrust in their eyes. You could tell they had no love for the Father and that they were wrapped up in their own importance and desires. Now and then she would get a glimpse into their eyes; they were full of lies and foolish pride. She felt her heart begin to tighten in anticipation of any ill will that might come her way from them. Her stomach began to knot, causing a wretched sickening. It was then that she noticed they too had a softness behind them. Unlike the crystal clear wings of the compassionate beings, these were a smoky gray with an occasional black sparkle.

A very handsome being emerged from their midst. It was obvious this was their leader. She felt a fearful attraction to him. He was so bold and dashing, and beautiful to behold, yet there was an icy coldness in his eye. She shivered involuntarily and stepped back as his gaze turned on her. She felt that he desired her. Her joy and hope began to disappear. Icy fingers of fear gripped her heart.

A drama began to unfold as the old ram continued to sing. She had no consciousness of him: only the story before her. The Great Father of Lights spoke in a thunder—a strong and awesome voice. As she returned her attention to the Father, the fingers of fear melted into nothingness. What was He saying?

Again His gentle thunder rolled as He spoke. It was almost like a purr that you felt could surely turn into a deafening roar at any moment. Finally, she focused in on what He was saying. They were all gazing down on a blue and green planet. As He spoke, varieties of horses came into being and were wafted to the planet on a breath from Him.

The whole assembly *ooh-ed* and *ahh-ed* at the magnificent spectacle of the horses racing swiftly on the winds of His breath to the jewel of a home awaiting them. As they ran, the Father spoke of a gift of wings much like their own so that one day the creatures might fly home to them and live among them for all eternity. Only those who spoke truth, showed love and compassion, and followed the ways of the Father would be given the gift of the wings.

It was then that the son of darkness spoke. (Now the Father knew that this one had become full of desire for power and had hopes of one day overthrowing Him.) Slyly, the son of darkness asked if the creatures might be given the choice of following the Father or himself.

Now it seemed obvious to most that the creatures would surely chose the peaceful, loving path of the Father. How could they possibly want to follow the evil ways of darkness?

At any rate, the Father agreed to give them a choice. What followed next seemed to greatly surprise the whole assembly. The Father in great anger thundered deafeningly:

"You have not the good of the creatures at heart, you think only of yourself and your evil lust for power! What you have asked grieves me deeply. I can no longer tolerate your presence among us. From this day forth you shall not set foot in this high place. I shall banish you from us to another planet until such time as I have prepared a permanent place for you and your followers."

The dark one made yet another request. "Until this place is prepared, allow us to dwell among the creatures that we might be allowed to persuade them, if we can, to follow us. How else could they possibly choose, except they are shown both sides?"

"As you wish!!!!"

With that the whole dark lot of them was dashed to earth on a lightening bolt, causing them much pain and discomfort.

Then the great Father turned solemnly and sadly to the remaining followers. "I fear the dark one shall try every manner of deception and temptation to keep the creatures from the gift I intended for them to have. He will take those things I meant for good and twist them so it appears to be the truth but is really only empty and selfish.

"He shall turn the giving of true and devoted love between one male and one female into a search for instant pleasure seeking among many partners and call it making love. The search for what they believe to be love will leave them empty, diseased, and alone.

"Though I have given them all they will ever need, he will take things that they don't need and call them riches. They will spend a lifetime of gathering, only to be leaving the stuff behind to weigh down their offspring. They and their offspring will spend so much time accumulating and guarding their 'riches' that they will not have time to seek the everlasting riches that I have prepared for them.

"Rather than following my ways and allowing my beautiful Spirit to fill them to overflowing with joy and deep peace, he shall fill them with his potions and drugs to control and rule their lives. He'll refer to this vile infilling of misery and enslaving substances as *partying* and the *happy hour*. In truth, they shall become miserable indeed having no control over their desire for the potions and become dull witted and empty of all joy.

"I will allow the creatures to make their choice. I shall send those of you who are willing as messengers to carry them my teachings. He shall seek to destroy all I send. Few will choose our ways. All will be led astray.

"I shall speak a deeper magic than he knows of and send forth a higher love of which he has no understanding. This will be at great cost to me, a thing his selfish heart will never understand. My love is great. In truth and purity it shall make a way for my creation to return to me. I love them more than he can comprehend. I myself shall pay the price for their wrongdoing. If they will but ask my forgiveness, I shall still send them the gift of my Spirit to fill them and restore them to fellowship with me. The Spirit shall teach them and help them to turn others back to me. At the appointed time, the Spirit shall bring them home to me.

"If my only Son, who is one with Me and My Spirit, will walk willingly as one of them and resist all temptations and teach them my ways, knowing full well that the son of darkness will have Him destroyed, then will the price be paid. You see, the dark one is only allowed to claim the lives of those who chose his ways. For Him to claim the life of one who has never erred breaks the agreement. Then I am free to claim back any that have sinned that will turn back to me.

"The dark one will be so intent on destroying my Son that he will not even think of the consequences of such an action on his part. With his own hands he shall destroy the eternal hold he hoped to have on the creatures. When he realizes his error, he shall redouble his efforts to keep them from knowing me or finding me. He will seek to enslave them in every way he can. My love shall overcome. My followers will suffer at his hands, but their reward shall be eternal and the riches of their souls everlasting. When all have made their choice, I shall hold the final judgment and bring my followers home and send the son of darkness and his followers into everlasting torment."

And it came to pass that the Son dwelt on the planet and walked as one of them but remained true to the Father. The day the dark one nailed Him to a tree thinking he had totally beaten the Father; he actually destroyed himself, for he had broken the deep magic and was guilty of taking what was not his. Now, he must pay the price.

Tears welled up in the young colt's eyes as the song ended. She stood transfixed. "What must I do to follow the

Father? I want to accept the Son's gift and receive the Father's Spirit." She spoke in hushed tones full of such deep emotion that she barely gave utterance; the emotion was so deep.

"You need only to ask the Father's forgiveness for the wrong you have done. Thank the Son for dying in your place and promise that from this day forth you will follow their ways and ask the Spirit of the Father to take control of your life and be your guide."

Quietly, the little colt looked at the twinkling lights high in the sky. She spoke ever so reverently and sincerely. "I saw your story. I know you are real. Please forgive me my wrongs; I want to follow your ways. I wish your Spirit to come into my heart and take over my life."

Such a gentle quiet joy as she had never known bathed her from inside out. Now she had a hope in her heart that would never die, for now truly, she was not alone. She was loved beyond measure. The night had been long. As she lay down to rest, she couldn't help but smile at the lights of the Father twinkling cheerily above her. They reminded her that even in seeming darkness, He ruled with His light.

The old ram stood watch over her until she nodded off and then he settled down for some rest himself. He lifted his lovely old face to the soft lights above and sighed peacefully. He spoke softly, "Yes, Father, another one will return home one day. Help me teach her to grow strong enough to see through the Darklord's tricks. May she stay on the path and show others the way to you. Send her the Spirit of Truth to help her."

Slowly, the old ram's head nodded until finally it rested on his chest. A gentle smile flitted across his face from time to time as moonbeams continued to play in his silvery white hair. His soft breathing changed to a soft comforting rumble.

Chapter Four

A playful ray of sunshine rippled over the wise old sheep and the young horse. It splashed merrily between the leaves dancing with the passing breeze. The warmth began to draw them back to consciousness. Softly, the little horse sighed and stretched, rousing from the land of dreams. Slowly, she opened her eyes to the waiting world. It was so peaceful and still, yet bustling with activity. A graceful doe and her fawn vanished into a thicket. A family of raccoons climbed sleepily up to their tree house. An old owl glided by on his way home.

A family of quail emerged from the brush in single file. The leader carefully looked around the clearing and called to find out where his cousins were. They answered with their throaty little, "I'm here!"

The lead quail then lowered his head into the charge position and dashed bravely across the clearing, following his perky little head feather. Upon reaching the other side, he called back, "I made it!"

One of the remaining group called out, "How is it?"

"I am safe!" was his reply. Promptly the remaining quail took the charge position and raced across the clearing, two and three at a time. Their jaunty little head banners led the way.

The old sheep had also roused from his sleep and noticed how intently the young colt was watching the quail. "What do you see?" queried the old sheep.

"I see some silly birds that are afraid to cross a clearing all at once."

"Hmmm," said the old sheep. "Is that all you see?"

"Well, I don't know. I think so," replied the colt. Deep inside she had a feeling he was after something else, but she wasn't sure what.

"I want you to think about what was going on. Now, tell me again what you saw."

"Well, OK. Some cute little birds came out to the edge of the brush. They called out to their cousins to see where they were at, and then only one raced across the clearing. Afterward, he called back that he was safe, the rest ran across." The colt tilted her head quizzically, looking to the old sheep for approval.

"Is that all you saw?" questioned the old ram.

"Well, earlier, I saw some raccoons going to sleep, and a deer disappearing into a thicket, and an old owl flying by." Surely the old ram would be greatly impressed at her great observation skills!

Slowly the old ram shook his head from side to side. "Look deeper, Child. Look deeper to the why, broader to the what, and higher to the pattern. Then add understanding and knowledge to the equation and you will begin to perceive what you have actually witnessed. There is a where and a who to consider as well. There is much more, but this is enough for now. In time even you will consider the all in all, and things not seen with your physical eyes. There are many kinds of sight. You have much to learn."

"I don't understand. If I see a bird running how can it be more than that?"

A gentle smile twitched into being, and ended in a soft chuckle. "Can you ask a why?"

"Sure, why was the bird running?"

"Now ask a what," said the old ram patiently.

"OK, what caused him to run instead of walk across the clearing?"

"Did you see any patterns?"

The little colt thought for a minute, "Hmmmm, well all the birds put their head in the same position to run."

"That's a start. Can you ask a where?"

"Where were they going? Hey, I think I'm getting it. Can I try?"

"Sure," chuckled the old ram.

"Why were they hiding in the brush? What made them hesitate? Why were the deer and raccoons bedding down to sleep? Why weren't the quail? Why did the owl fly by? Where had the deer been? Why were the raccoons tired? Why did some hide in grasses and others in trees? Why did they hide at all? Who made them? What do they eat?"

"OK, OK, slow down," the old ram chuckled. "Now, if you find the answers to your questions, and observe how it all works together, you will have the tools to bring about understanding and wisdom. When you have achieved these two things, then everything will speak to you. There are great mysteries and truths all about us if we could truly see and hear."

"I'll never know all there is to know!" she sighed.

"Already you have the beginning of true wisdom," whispered the old ram. "A few minutes ago you were proud of all you had seen."

The little colt sheepishly hung her head. It was true; she had even expected praise!

"Now, I see humility has replaced your pride, and you have found a deep hunger to learn rising within you."

"I want to know all about everything then," she said determinedly.

"Hmmm, to know without understanding is as empty as seeing without asking questions. If you know everything about everything, but do not understand how it all works together, then you only know. If you can gain understanding on many levels, and see many truths, then you have the beginning of wisdom. With even a small amount of wisdom comes true humility. The more you learn and understand, the more you know that you don't know much."

"When will I ever get wisdom?" asked the colt, slightly exasperated.

"That comes in time, Child. Some things come quickly, and others take a lifetime. Part of that depends on if you truly seek and desire it."

"I do desire wisdom!" she passionately declared.

"There are two kinds of wisdom," said the old sheep matter-of-factly. "There is a way that seems wise to the student, and there is the wisdom of the Father."

"What's the difference?" she questioned.

"Well, the student's wisdom comes from his understanding of what he thinks he knows. The Father, who created all and has a higher plan, has a wisdom that is based on what is eternal and everlasting. His wisdom is not understood by those who only see what is before them."

"I'm not sure I understand the difference."

"Hmmm, I'll try to help you some. Where did you come from?"

"The land of dark mists," she replied.

"Why are you the only one who came?"

"I don't know."

"Think now."

"OK, the rest all have horrid collars on their necks and can't leave. Also they have to work hard so they can have food and a place to stay. The dragons have to guard the treasures and keep them safe."

"Where is your collar?"

"My mom chewed it off."

"Why didn't any other collars get chewed off?"

"Well, if they don't have the collars, they can't work, and can't have a place to stay or eat."

"Are you hungry?" asked the old ram.

"Nooo . . ."

"Do you have a place to sleep?"

"Well, yes and no. Not a set place or a barn, but I sleep just fine!" she exclaimed, a light beginning to dawn.

"Do you like where you are or where you were?"

"Definitely here!"

"Did you know this was here till you came?"

"Well, not exactly. We heard stories about someplace different."

"Now that you're here, is this what you thought it was like."

"Not even close! I'd heard about deep grass, and warm sunshine and clear waters, but I didn't know what they were. I never saw them before. How could I know?"

"And all the others, do they like where they are?"

"That's hard. I don't think they're happy, but they think that's all there is."

"Do they look forward to anything?"

"I don't think so, but I don't know what that means," answered the little colt, unsure of her answer.

"Is there something wonderful they think about and expect to happen? Is there something that makes them glad to be alive? Do they smile and sing and laugh?"

"No. There is only sadness. Everything is dark and dreary. Some go to the neon houses, but they aren't happy either. No. There is nothing wonderful. They just live and eat and work and die."

"Did they hear the stories of the flying horses?"

"Yes, but they don't think they're true. They were afraid that if they left, they would not be fed or have a place to live. They were afraid they would lose their jobs."

"So, what you are saying is that there is a way to live that seems right to the others based on their understanding of what they think is real. Is that correct?"

"Well, yes."

"That is the wisdom of the world. You, on the other hand, wanted to believe the stories, even though you weren't sure. You went in search of the truth." The old ram paused, full of thought. "Do you remember the first time you began to think something wonderful might happen on your journey?"

"Yes, yes! When I woke in the field of grass and felt a ray of light! I got excited because I found something I'd heard about that was actually true. That was when I got excited, because I thought that maybe the flying horses were real too!" exclaimed the colt.

"That is called hope," stated the old ram gently.

"After that, it didn't seem to matter so much how hard it was to climb this mountain. I just had to find the flying horses I'd heard about."

"With hope comes determination. Come, Little One, I want you to meet a friend of mine." Quietly, the two walked over to a tender sapling. There on one of the leaves was a fat, striped caterpillar. He was chomping and chewing on a leaf. He had such a tiny mouth. All of his bites were itsy bitsy. "Good morning, Friend. I see you are hard at work."

"Oh yes!" sang out the caterpillar.

"Well, would you mind telling our new friend here what you will be doing in a few weeks?"

"Sure! I shall soar and fly from flower to flower, and go on many grand adventures!"

The young horse began to laugh uncontrollably. She was laughing so hard, that tears came. It was even hard to stand; her body was shaking so hard. Soon, she started gasping for extra breath. Oh, what a ridiculous thought! This fat, striped creature flying through the air! It had no wings! How could it fly? Oh, it was just too funny for words. Finally, she managed to gain some control. Tremors of suppressed laughter rippled through her as she fought valiantly for control.

Tears welled up in the little caterpillar's eyes. It cast its gaze down, and then turned to the old ram. Its lower lip began to tremble into a sad little frown, and it choked back a sob. Raising its eyes to the ram, and bravely blinking back tears it whispered, "I will fly, you know."

Suddenly the little horse felt very sorry she had laughed. The little caterpillar turned sadly back to her. With determination he whispered, "I will fly." The old ram nodded a knowing yes. At that, the little caterpillar breathed in peace and exhaled his pain.

The old ram turned sadly to the colt. "You've hurt my friend. You laugh at what you do not understand. Is it any easier to believe that a huge creature like yourself can fly?"

"I'm sorry, Little Friend," said the horse. "It's just that . . . well . . . you don't have any wings that I can see."

The little caterpillar tilted his head back and to one side. "They're inside my heart. One day after I've learned more and grown more, what's in my heart will become visible. I was promised that if I followed the ways of the Father of Lights, that one day I would fly!"

"I was promised that too! I'm beginning my journey to find the secret of the flying horses. I want to follow the way of the True Light." The little horse moved her head closer to the caterpillar and whispered, "I want to fly too, but I don't know where or how I'll ever get wings."

"Maybe they're in your heart, too," whispered the caterpillar.

"Do you really think so?" asked the horse hopefully. Together they turned to the old ram for answers.

He was smiling fondly at the two new friends. "You are learning much from each other. That is good. Many questions are in your hearts, and answers I could give. However, if I only gave answers, you may not truly know or understand what I have said. It is better that you learn by the living and doing. These lessons will be written in your heart, not just your head. There are some that have tried to learn by just asking questions. They can tell you the answers. They can describe all they have heard and how they think it should happen. But they have never flown.

"To only know in your head, but not have it written in your whole being, is to be without life and will only produce much knowledge. Many become so proud of their knowledge that they have forgotten to gain higher wisdom. They have forgotten the *why*, the *what*, the *how* and the *be* of the teachings. They have become wise in their own eyes and perceive that they are better than the others are. They tell the others to learn the knowledge and be like them. The world sees nothing wonderful in the knowledge of flying. Since they have never actually done it, they have decided that the whole idea must not be true."

"I truly wish to fly, not just know how to. Please help me know how to do this," said the little horse.

"Follow me," said the old ram. "I will be your guide."

And with that, they said goodbye to the caterpillar and wished him the joy of flight.

Chapter Five

The old ram led the little horse back to the edge of the forest. Before them was the great white mist and the steep narrow trail going down, down, down, till it totally disappeared. On the other side of the mist were the beautiful lands where she had seen the flying horses. She began to shiver with excitement. The old ram slowly turned and looked questioningly into her eyes. "Will you follow me down the narrow path?" he asked.

"Oh yes!" she sang out.

Tenderly, he looked at her. She was so full of enthusiasm. "Stay close, do as I say, and all will be well. There are some dangerous sections, but if you stay on the path and follow me, you will make it safely through."

Slowly and deliberately, the old ram began his descent. Gladly, the little colt followed. She was so excited at the prospect of seeing the flying horses. Nothing fazed her. Once in awhile she would skid on some loose stones, but always managed to maintain her balance.

At first, she could see the ram fairly well. As they descended, she found it harder and harder to make out his form. His whiteness blended into the whiteness of the mist. Suddenly she panicked, she wasn't totally sure of where the ram was. "I can't see you!" she cried out frantically. Her eyes tried desperately to pierce the mists, but to no avail. Everything looked the same. "I want to follow you, but how am I supposed to do that if I can't see you?" Her voice was full of desperation.

"Can you see my feet?" the wise old ram patiently queried.

She glanced down to where his feet might be. Yes, she could see his feet! "I can!" she called out as relief flooded through her.

"Can you hear my voice?" he asked.

"Yes, I can hear your voice," she called out with a little more confidence. Her strength was coming back.

"Here's what you are to do," said the old ram. "Put your feet where you saw mine last. Focus on my steps and listen to my voice. If we are making a turn, I will tell you. I will give you instructions as we go."

They walked on for a little way. The colt intently watched the ram's shiny black hooves. She listened to his voice with all her might. Her eyes stayed glued to his feet and her ears stayed tuned in to his voice. It didn't seem to matter so much what was around them. The ram knew the way, and she knew he would get them to their destination. His voice had become a great comfort. They continued to talk as they journeyed forward. As they were walking and talking she began to wonder about something.

"How do you know where to go?" she questioned.

The old ram chuckled softly. "You are learning to ask questions. That is good," he said smiling to himself. "This is a tough question."

"I want to know!" she said passionately.

"OK, let's see. Do you remember about the different kinds of wisdom?"

"Yes," she said slowly, pondering the earlier lesson. "There is the wisdom that the horses in the shadow land had, based on what they believed to be true. Then there is a higher wisdom based on the Father's truth."

"Very good. You learn quickly. Do you remember about seeing things two ways?" he asked tentatively.

"Well, you can see what is right in front of you without knowing the why, how, what and where of it. You can also see with an understanding of all that you see," she replied slowly, as her mind searched for answers.

"Excellent," replied the old ram, his voice gently falling off into thought. He continued, "There are things you can see with your physical eyes that seem real and are actually only temporary. There are things you can see with your heart and your spirit and not your physical eyes that will last forever."

The little colt looked puzzled. "If I can't see something, how can it be real? How will I know it is there?"

"Can you see the wind?"

"No."

"How do you know it is there?" he asked.

"I can see what it does," she said, deep in thought. Her brow furrowed with intensity.

"Can you see me as I walk in front of you through the mists?"

"I only see your feet."

"Am I there, though you do not see me?"

"Well, yes," she answered.

"How do you know what to do?" he asked.

"I listen to your voice and obey what you say. I stay focused on where you walk so that I'll know where to walk."

"Do you know more now than you did before you began your journey from the shadow lands?"

"Oh, yes!" she sang out, enthusiastically.

"Is the world bigger or smaller now that you've traveled?"

"It is the same; I've just seen more and learned more."

He questioned her further. "The things you have not yet seen . . . are they real or not?"

She thought for a moment. "They are real, but I don't know about them yet."

"And . . . do you see in your mind the places you have never been? Do you feel them in your heart?"

Slowly she shook her head from side to side, still deep in thought. "Nooo."

"Do you see in your mind all the places you have been?"

"Oh, yes!"

"Hmmm, well, there are things you do not understand right now. The mists through which we now walk are of another dimension. You cannot see through them because you are just beginning your journey. As you grow and learn and talk with the Father, you will hear His voice and he will open your inner eyes to the things that are forever. You will gain understanding of higher things, and the mists will no longer be there for you, even as they no longer exist for me. Understanding will clarify your sight."

"What about the dark mists where I came from? What were they?" she asked, feeling that there was some possible connection.

"Look in your heart for the answer. The Father's Spirit is already teaching you, or you would not have asked the question. Listen to what He puts in your heart." The old ram let her ponder a bit. "You don't have to think so hard, Little One, beware of trying to think too much or the answer might only be of your own making. Hear the Father's voice within your heart: Be still and listen."

Quietly they plodded on, the old ram softly humming and the colt concentrating on his steps and voice. She felt in her heart that perhaps the dark mists had to do with a lack of understanding too. She would try to listen to the Father and learn from Him. New questions were welling up within her. Was that the Father's Spirit leading her to a better understanding? A few days ago she would not have asked the things that now begged for answers.

Eventually her mind quieted and focused on the task at hand. She was beginning to get hungry. Her stomach began rumbling and growling at her. It would be so nice to have some of the rich green grasses they had eaten that morning. The mists were still there, though she had begun to find them more comforting than frightening. The ram's footsteps rhythmically resounded on the stones. Her mind began to relax, as her body stayed in sync with the ram's movements. Her eyes remained glued to his steps, yet it no longer required extreme concentration. It became easier to follow him, almost a natural thing.

As she relaxed she found her mind able to focus on the ram's voice more easily. The tune he was humming was hauntingly beautiful. It was joyful yet sad, strong and tender, courageous and hopeful. Listening made her feel like laughing and crying, rushing into battle and resting in safe comfort, striving against all odds to overcome and the sweet assurance that she would reach her destination. What a strange tune, she thought to herself. Soon, she found herself humming effortlessly along with the ram. Forgotten was the rumbling in her belly; her mind was satisfied; her body felt warm and good with the steady motion.

Suddenly the ram called out, "Hard right!" She stepped where he had been and whirled hard to her right. She could still see his hoofs and felt secure. Again he called out, "Listen only to my voice!" Soon she began to hear strange noises, really strange noises! What could they be? Then she remembered, the ram's command: "Listen only to my voice." Out of the mists she heard his tune and saw his feet. As long as she listened only to his voice she felt calm. Those other noises tugged at her mind once again. She concentrated on their strangeness. Fear began to rise within her. There were so many noises! What if they belonged to something that could eat her?

She began to strain her eyes, looking into the mists towards the sounds. She had forgotten everything—the beautiful flying horses, the wise old ram, and the hopeful caterpillar. Everything vanished from her mind. She forgot where she was going; who she was following, and his instructions. A terrifying confusion engulfed her, trying to swallow her whole. Where were the ram's feet? Where was his voice?

"Help me!" she cried out in desperation, refusing to move another step. Confusion swirled around her at a dizzying pace. Perhaps it was all a mistake. Why had she ever followed the ram? Maybe he really didn't know where he was going and they were lost forever. Again she cried out, "Please, please help me!"

Once again the old ram emerged from the mists before her. Sadly he shook his head, and gently he nuzzled her, comforted her. The once proud little head hung down to her knees. The flesh seemed to hang from her bones. She felt ashamed that she had not followed his simple instructions. All he had asked her to do was to listen to his voice and to follow his steps. He had told her he would guide her safely through. He had warned her that there would be dangers. Perhaps he would lose patience with her and take her home instead of on a wonderful journey. Oh, how she wished she could start all over and get it right! Why had she thought it would be so easy to follow? She couldn't even follow two simple instructions!

The old ram whispered softly to the young colt's aching heart. "Fear not. I am here, and I love you. Follow me and I will lead you safely to your destination. You must trust me and know that I understand and see those things that you cannot. I will lead you safely through."

A great big tear rolled down her face and splashed to the ground. Soon a little river of tears trickled down her face and cascaded to the thirsty ground. "I'm so sorry," she murmured. "Please forgive me."

"All is forgiven, Child. I see your heart and know your desire. Come, follow me and learn the ways of the Father. He is patient and loving and kind. He is always with us. We are never alone. If we listen to His voice He will comfort and guide us through the worst of situations."

"Thank you." she whispered gratefully. The pain in her heart lessened. A stronger determination was rising within. She *would* follow the Father and listen to His voice. She *would* find the horses that flew and perhaps find wings of her own. A flicker of fear passed through her as she listened again to the sounds. "Why are the noises so frightening to me and not to you?"

"Child, you are growing quickly to have noticed that there is no fear in my heart. The Father has given you a gift; use it wisely and He will show you the simplicity of the mysteries of life. So many see complexities and miss the obvious. Most are too busy to be still and listen to His voice in their heart." The old ram rubbed his chin thoughtfully.

"What is my gift? I don't understand," she asked humbly.

"When others speak you will hear the words of their heart as loudly as the words of their mouth. You will hear what is not said as clearly as the spoken word. You will not see limitations as clearly as you see possibilities. You will know the truth."

"How did you get all of that from my question?"

"To ask such a question while you were feeling fear shows that you realize what is going on in someone else. You are not consumed by your own emotion. The Father's Spirit within you has revealed to you a greater possibility than what exists within yourself. Then you acted on what He had shown you. Listen to His discerning Spirit within your heart and believe that above all else. His truth is everlasting and to walk with Him into the unknown at His command is safer than a known way. The key is to always listen to Him and follow His voice.

"The other noises you heard were only distractions sent by the Darklord to try and get you to turn back or at least halt your progress. They have no real power over one who belongs to the Father. The Son's life paid the price.

"It makes the Father sad when we forget and focus on our fears rather than His love for us. Fear is an immobilizer. It halts our journey. When we feel afraid from time to time it helps to remember to trust the Father's love. The things around us have no power over us unless we give them our full attention. That is the Darklord's only hope to keep us from doing the will of the Father. It is his hope to prevent us from discovering our freedom and from leading others to their freedom.

"There is a battle going on that you will one day see clearly. Now is not the time to discuss those things. Come; let's be on our way! We're almost to the Great Desert!" The old ram thought a minute. "You know, it's always been my experience that the closer you get to your goal the harder the Darklord tries to distract you. It's funny in a way, but I have almost come to welcome those attacks. It now serves as an encouragement rather than a discouragement because I know the goal is almost in sight! So many stop just short of the bounty and joys the Father desired to share with them because they stopped one day too soon."

"I will never stop!" she declared.

"Oh, Child, I pray not. The Darklord uses other things to draw our focus from the Father's will. He doesn't always use fears. From time to time he'll use things that by appearance seem good and wonderful. It is critical to keep your heart and mind and soul focused on His Voice only."

The two walked on into the mists. The strange noises were now only an indistinguishable rumble around her. Only the voice of the ram was clear, for that was what she chose to listen to. Only his feet did she gaze upon. Her heart was at peace, and the joy of the journey returned. After all, the Father loved her and she was on her way to find the flying horses!

The trail rose before them. Their steps became more labored and deliberate. Rumbling background noises urgently begged for her attention, but to no avail. She had set her heart and mind on the task before her and trusted the counsel of the ram and the Spirit within. They must be nearing their destination! She would make it, she would!

Suddenly the mists began to thin. She could see the great golden mesas rising before her. They had made it! Gleefully she scrambled up the remaining trail. Wow! Oh, how her heart ached with the joy of it all. Lifting her head and her heart to the glorious skies and beauty around her, words of thankfulness rose from her heart. "Thank you, Father! Oh thank you, so very, very much." Tears of joy washed through her and splashed to the sands below.

The old ram had found a resting place in the shelter of the rocks. Their eyes met in quiet victory. Yes, it was good. They had survived and reached their destination. As she relaxed, a delicious weariness flooded through her. *Ummm*, a nap would feel absolutely wonderful. She lay down near the ram and succumbed quickly to a deep and restful sleep. Visions of white mists and the ram's feet and his haunting song gently swirled through her dreams.

Chapter Six

Gnawing hunger pains roused her from the realm of rest and dreams. Wow, was she ever hungry! She looked for the ram. He had already risen and was bending over a strange green plant. Quickly she raced to his side. The plant had dangerous looking spikes all over it. She gently touched one. "Ouch! That hurt!"

Chuckling softly the old ram asked her a question. "What do you see?"

"I see a mean old sticker plant!" she retorted, still smarting from its dagger. "What do you see?"

"Hmmm," mused the old one. "I see a plant that has managed to survive a harsh arid climate. It protects its vital parts from predators with its thorns. Even though there is little water and nourishment for itself, it still manages to share with others without endangering itself."

"What is it sharing? Pain?"

"No, Little One. You have focused only on one aspect of the plant. Look at the soft red bulb it holds up to you.

The spines on the red fruit are soft. You may eat this without endangering its life."

"Oh," she humbly replied.

They ate their fill of the juicy fruits. Oh YUM! These were wonderful. She thanked the little plant for sharing. A new appreciation and respect replaced her former dislike.

"Remember to look for the good in all things and you will find it. Do not judge quickly; do not judge at all. Seek the beauty and secrets of life and they will be shown to you. What you look for is what you will see. Look beyond the outside to the heart of all things. Many only find the thorns of life and miss its sweetness." The old ram stopped and thought a moment. "Always look with your heart, and the Spirit will reveal truth and wisdom to you."

They walked over to the beautiful desert stream and drank deeply of its waters. Now she was anxious to see the flying horses! She looked expectantly at the old ram. He was gazing peacefully at the golden beauty around him. She joined him in his repose. The desert seemed to fill her heart and soul with its strength and beauty. Great rocks rose majestically out of the sea of sand, sentinels of the desert, mighty and glorious. Soft green clouds of sage dotted the great expanse before them. Great cacti lifted their arms to the heavens while the smaller varieties squatted close to the earth. Occasionally, a graceful hawk would soar by, circling in search of food. Nearby a light brown lizard scampered by.

"Will we see the flying horses today?" asked the little colt. She was enjoying the beauty, but anxious to get on with the journey. "I want to learn the secret of their power to fly!"

"Hmmm," mused the old ram. "So you would like to discover their power?"

"Oh, yes!" she replied excitedly.

The old ram reached into his embroidered traveling bag and pulled out a soft, little violet pouch on a long silken cord. It looked like there was something in it. "Here, Little One, take this amulet." He slipped the silken cord over her neck.

"What is this for? Will it give me great powers?" she asked.

"Hmm. If you discover the secret of what is in it you will have found great wisdom. That wisdom will allow you to receive all the power you will ever need."

"That sounds like a riddle. What's in the pouch?" she inquired.

"Dust." He spoke the word solemnly.

"Dust?" She couldn't believe it. Was he kidding her? "You mean to tell me that if I find the secret of dust I will be wise?"

Slowly he nodded his head.

"You're serious about this, aren't you? Am I really supposed to go on a quest to find the secret of dust?"

"I speak the truth, Child. Sometimes, what appears foolish is great wisdom. Only those seeking wisdom will find it. It is there for all to see, but not all will find it. I will camp here by this great rock. I have need of time alone with the Father. You may go on your quest in any direction. Keep this rock in sight and return in the evening. The river is near to quench your thirst, and the cactus fruits and scattered grasses will give you nourishment."

"OK, here I go in a quest for the mystery of dust." She muttered sarcastically under her breath. This seemed so foolish.

Ambling along, she began to speak to the dust, as if it would answer her questions. "Hmm. Well dust, what are your secrets? You are beneath my feet. I step on you, and it doesn't hurt you. You just lay there. You don't talk or hear. Surely that's not the secret."

She spent most of the day in silence, looking at the dust. From time to time she looked back to be sure she could see the great rock near their camp. Sometimes she noticed that the dust was in a rippled pattern, like so many waves, but still it just lay there. Every now and then she'd give it a gentle kick and it would scatter before her. She noticed that a lot of the sand was piled up against the large rocks, but she wasn't sure why. Maybe that's where it had always been, or maybe that's where it came from. There was even some dust in little cracks and crevices in the rock. How did it get there? She stared at it for a long time but nothing happened.

The sun was beginning to set, and she was getting hungry. Quickly, she raced to the river for a long drink. She munched some of the tasty cactus fruits and headed for the rock. What would she tell the old ram? She hadn't learned a thing all day long! She saw him watching for her as she approached. It was nice to have his sweet old friendly face to greet her.

"Good evening, Child. I see you listened well and have found your way back safely." He smiled warmly at her.

Well, she had followed his instructions today. That at least was an improvement from the trip through the mists. She deeply appreciated his noticing her effort.

Much to her relief, the old ram said, "Let us rest and think on the things we have learned today. We will discuss them in the morning."

Silently they watched the sun bathe the golden rocks in hues of red and violet. It was breathtaking. Watching it for the first time she felt so small and yet so large all at once. Deep joy rose from her heart and shone through her eyes. The old one noticed and smiled.

The colors faded and a velvety darkness lay over the land. Twinkling stars began to appear until the sky was covered in their splendor. The whole sky shimmered above them like a jewel-studded blanket. Eventually, they drifted off to sleep while the planet effortlessly carried them to yet another day.

Once in the land of dreams, the young colt saw sand everywhere! She saw piles of sand, ripples of sand, sand on the rocks, sand on her feet, sand was everywhere she turned! Soon the scenes of sand were whirling and swirling around her. She woke with a start. It was morning. Everything was still and beautiful.

"Good morning, Child," said the old ram warmly.

"Good morning, Old One," replied the colt with much respect.

"What did you learn yesterday?" questioned the ram.

She had been dreading this moment, but bravely spoke her truth. "I learned that dust can't do anything. It just lies there."

"You have the beginning of wisdom," spoke the old ram softly.

Her eyes opened wide in unbelief and she began to laugh. "Oh, I can hear it now. She knows dust can't do anything, she is *sooo* wise. Tell us again, O' wise one. What does dust do? Nothing! Wow!"

"Child," he spoke gently and smiled shaking his head softly from side to side. "Did you hear my words? I said you have the beginning of wisdom. You are only right in part. There is wisdom far deeper than this that can only be seen with the eyes of your spirit. Look deeper, much deeper to that which your physical eyes cannot see."

"I shall try." Quietly, she turned and walked away, pondering the depths of dust and shaking her head. The wind began to blow, gently at first. It toyed with her mane and gently pushed the grains of sand. She saw some interesting rocks she'd like to explore and headed towards them. The winds became stronger and stronger. She raced towards the rocks hoping to find shelter from the stinging sands! Ouch, they hurt! There was a break in the rocks. She ducked into it and discovered a quiet grotto. Outside she could hear the sands pounding the rocks. She mused, "Dust can't do anything, but the wind can use it in powerful ways. Dust used by the wind can carve mountains!"

She looked around in her sheltered cove. Over in a corner she saw a crumbling skeleton surrounded by sand. Suddenly there came a solemn dawning. "I was made from dust, I will return to dust. It is the life from the Father of Lights that gives me power. Without Him I am but dust."

Her old mentor appeared from nowhere. "Yes, Child. He breathes life into us. Just as the wind can carve a mountain, He can do mighty things with us if we surrender to His will. Wear the amulet as a reminder of your need for Him."

"I will," she solemnly replied.

They spent the rest of the day weathering the storm in the grotto. The old ram had picked some of the cactus fruits and brought them in his pouch. They snacked and spoke of the Father's wisdom. That night the wind died down, and the desert air chilled. Reaching into his traveling pouch the old ram pulled out a fire stick and his tinderbox. They gathered loose brush and made a respectable little pile. Skillfully the ram sparked it into life, blowing gently on the smoldering coal from his box. Quickly the fire stick burst into flame. The flame ran merrily to all the dry wood leaping and flaring into a warm, crackling fire. It was cozy and beautiful. Lights from the fire danced eerily on the surrounding walls. Lost in thought, the two travelers gazed at the comforting flames.

"Please tell me about the desert horses," the young colt asked quietly.

"Hmmm," mused the old ram. "That is a longer story than I have time to tell tonight. I will tell you the story of one particularly hard winter." The old ram stirred the fire and added a bit more brush. It leapt quickly, flashing and flickering, pushing back the darkness. The two companions nestled down beside it as the ram began his tale.

"Long, long ago on a cold desert night, a dark, mysterious stranger came to this land. It had been a particularly hard winter. Grasses were hard to find. A cold blanket of snow hid them from view. The horses had to paw through the snow in search of the life-giving grass. Often, they would paw through and find only sand. Their energy was running low. Without proper nourishment it became harder and harder to search for the grasses. The dark stranger brought them a load of hay and left."

"Now, the hay was surely a welcome sight. The Old Ones stayed back warily scouting the horizons. They wondered why the hay had been brought. All of the youngsters rushed in and ate hungrily. They didn't care why it was there, they were hungry and here was food! When the Old Ones saw that nothing happened to the others, they ate also, but warily.

"The dark stranger came every day leaving them food and going away. Now, no one went foraging for food. They just stayed close to where they were being fed. Their bodies began to go soft from lack of exercise. Bickering broke out among them. Their excess energy had no outlet; it flared and snapped at each other. Some fought over whom would eat first. Others tried to hoard some for later, just in case the stranger didn't come.

"One day they noticed that some poles had been put up near the hay. The youngsters didn't care. What were a few poles? It didn't interfere with their eating. Several of the older and wiser horses began to worry. They wished their leader and the scouts would return from their search for better grazing. More poles appeared on the following day. The elders called a meeting.

"The oldest and wisest horse spoke. 'I don't like the changes I see in our herd. We are no longer strong and free. We lay around waiting for hay to be delivered rather than find our own grasses. Yes, it was hard, but we were strong and tough. What little we had we shared. Now we have much and bicker all day. We have no purpose. I do not like this life; it does not feel right. Tonight, I am leaving in search of the leader and the scouts. I do not like the poles; something is not right. I've seen enough. Why would someone give us food day after day? I do not know this dark stranger or his motives. I say, let us leave now before it is too late! Who will go with me?'

"Several of the older horses followed and a few of the younger ones. About half of the herd stayed. They were tired of hunting for food. Most of them agreed that nothing could be worse than not having food in their bellies. They would take their chances.

"That night, the freedom lovers left. They trekked for many days towards the purple mountains. Gradually, their bodies grew strong again from the struggle. Enough grasses were found to keep them alive. On the fifth day they saw a small band of horses approaching them. It was their leader. He had found rich grazing beneath the snows of the foothills! The old wise horse told them what had happened back in the desert. Two of the scouts were sent to get the others. The rest of them followed their leader to the new grazing land.

"When the scouts arrived at the feeding area they found a strange sight. There was only a circle of poles around some sparse bits of hay, but no horses! There was a well trodden trail leading to the treacherous canyon. The scouts followed the trail through the canyon and up to the thick forest. It disappeared into the woods. The weary scouts rested, ate some of the lush grasses and returned to the foothills. The band of horses that left were never heard of again.

"The day after the scouts returned, the oldest, wisest horse had a vision. He said that before all truth perishes, a horse would come through the mists from the dark side. The spark of truth will grow and become a shining light. That light will go into the darkness and show many the path home."

Silently the eyes of the colt and the ram met. They both knew it had come to pass. There was much to learn before she journeyed back to the dark side. The blazing fire flooded the grotto with light, and drew their thoughts to the path before them. Gradually they drifted off to sleep. Tomorrow she would see the desert horses!

Chapter Seven

It was morning! Excitement rippled through her in luscious waves. She could hardly wait to see the flying horses! The old ram was already up and eating some of the sparse but tasty grasses. Quickly, she rushed to his side. "How long until we see the horses?" she asked, her voice quivering with excitement.

"It will be soon, Child. There is a hidden valley not far from here. We shall journey there today." He smiled softly at her bubbling enthusiasm. Both were deep in thought as they munched some of the cactus fruits.

Finally, they began their trek. The sun's warm rays felt so pleasant and cheery. The light seemed to reach her innermost parts. Everything was hushed . . . almost as if time stood still and only the two of them moved forward across the unchanging sands. The vast stillness gradually seeped through her whole being like calm water. Soon, her heart and mind became quiet as well. She could feel her body moving and hear her own breathing . . . but it seemed distant. It was almost as if she were observing her own movements from a stationary lookout.

Thoughts seemed to float effortlessly through her whole being—not anything that she could pinpoint but an unconscious flood of thoughts. They ebbed and flowed like a tide, washing through her entirety. Sands of her existing thoughts were stirred up with their action and subtly changed. Her thoughts were like pebbles being cleaned and polished by the waters of thoughts passing over them. She felt tuned in to every plant, animal, grain of sand, the seen and the unseen. A quiet voice inside began to emerge and seemed to radiate quiet truths and bits of wisdom. The voice itself wasn't separate from the vast quietness. It was the center of it.

She was so absorbed in the thoughts coursing through her that she hadn't noticed the distant dark flying objects. Suddenly, the quiet fled, chased away by a deep uneasiness. The voice inside urged her quietly, "Run to the canyons. Quickly, Little One. Run!"

Her feet seemed to fly as she sped past the old ram into the nearby canyon. Looking back over her shoulder, she saw the dragon scouts in the distance. She had forgotten all about the former dreariness and dark existence. Now, as she sped into the golden maze of stone, it all came flooding back. Soon the ram was by her side. Together they scurried forward through the narrow break in the stone. She felt weak and nauseated. It was as if she had been internally wounded. *Why does my life have to be interrupted by the meanness and ugliness of the dragon scouts? Why do they have to show up right before I get to see the desert horses? It just isn't fair!*

She and the ram followed the narrow winding path. Suddenly, it opened onto a broad grassy meadow. A band of wild horses was racing to the far end of the canyon. Swiftly they raced with their necks stretched out, feet flying, manes and tails streaming behind them. They were so powerful, so glorious and strong! Quickly, they vanished into a break in the canyon wall.

"NOOOOO!" she screamed! "Noooooo! Come back!"

They were too far away and traveling so fast that she would never catch them. Truly, they were gone.

"Now what?" she wailed mournfully to the old ram, momentarily forgetting the dragon scouts. "Will I ever see the flying horses?"

Deep in thought, she suddenly stopped and turned to the ram. Softly she whispered, "Those horses weren't flying. I saw no wings."

"Hmmm," said the old ram.

Quizzically, she looked into his face, but he said no more. A heavy disappointment was settling over her heart and she began to doubt that the flying horses existed. Perhaps it hadn't been a horse she'd seen soaring in the mountains. Perhaps it had only been a very large bird and she had just wanted for it to be a horse so badly that it appeared to be!

The old ram brought her back from the heavy thoughts to their own danger. "I think we should stay here in the canyon till nightfall and cross the open meadow in the dark."

"Huh? What are you talking about?" asked the colt, still pondering her recent disappointment.

Patiently, the ram replied. "The dragon scouts, Child, they're seeking something. They haven't come this far in a very long time. That is why the desert horses fled. I'm sure they're racing to the safety of the purple mountains. I'm sorry you didn't get to meet them."

Dejected, she looked down at the ground. Under her breath she muttered, "They had no wings."

"Are you certain?" queried the ram.

"I didn't see any wings, and they only ran," she replied dismally.

"Have you forgotten so quickly all you have learned?"

"What are you talking about? What did I learn about the flying horses running?" she retorted.

"Hmmmm. Well, do you know why they were running and not flying? Are things only so because you see them, or are there things that exist that you can't see? You still have much to learn. The Spirit within you will teach you. Hear His voice; trust what He says. He will write the Father's wisdom and truth into your soul."

"Why can't you teach me this?"

"It has come to me that I need to return to the Shadowland. The Darklord is feeling his reign threatened. He'll do everything he can to destroy that threat," replied the old ram, deep in thought.

"What could possibly threaten him?"

"The Truth, the Light, and the power of Love. You are now a threat to him."

"How can that be?" she laughed.

"If one who knows the truth and is filled with the Light of the Father goes in love to share that truth in the land of darkness, the darkness will disappear. His power over the horses only exists if they believe his lies. You represent the light and truth. He will fight you in every way possible to turn you from leading the others to the truth. There is a hard choice that you must make now. Will you continue to pursue the desert horses or will you return to the land of darkness and take the light and truth and pass it on to others? The Darklord will be hunting for you and seeking to turn you from your mission. He cannot destroy you for you belong to the Father, but he will try to entice you away from your true destiny.

"One choice will bring satisfaction to you at seeing the great flying ones and learning from them. Your other choice will mean existing in a dark land while attempting to give others hope and a path out of the darkness. If you make this choice, it may be awhile before you see the desert horses. The reward of bringing others with you to find them might prove even more rewarding."

A big lump caught in her throat as she considered the choices. Oh, how she wanted to stay in this beautiful land of sun, golden rocks, crystal clear streams, and violet mountains. Returning now to the gray fog and sadness seemed heavy and oppressive. She thought of the others—her mother, and the young colts crying. Her heart told her she must go back. She would sacrifice her own desires to help the others. Perhaps in time, she could return and go to the mountains in quest of the flying ones. Perhaps in time . . .

"I'll go back," she whispered quietly, not trusting her voice. She wanted to cry. Deep within her heart was a good cry longing to break past the barriers she had placed around it.

"You do have a choice," spoke the ram. "Either would be pleasing to the Father."

"I want to go back," she said, trying to convince herself more than anything. Deep inside, she was feeling every bit the martyr. She hoped the ram and the Father were pleased with her sacrifice. She hoped those in the shadow land appreciated what she was giving up to help them.

The old ram looked deep into her heart. Finally he said, "It is good. I myself must return and see what is going on in the dark land. I will lead you through the mists."

They found a hollow in the canyon wall and rested until nightfall. Together they trekked back to the trail in the mists. Her eyes stayed focused on the ram's feet, but her heart was churning with conflict. She didn't want to leave the beautiful land full of light and peace. Yet, a strange excitement rumbled inside. It was almost as if a battle cry were sounding. "Forward and onward! Set my children free!" A determination was rising from within her. A strength she couldn't fully understand began to permeate her whole being. Perhaps she could make a difference. An unexplainable joy began to fill her heart and add to her strength.

She contemplated these things. Here she was, walking back to dreariness and pain, yet she felt so strong and alive and full of joy that she could hardly contain it. What was happening? Maybe this wouldn't be so bad after all! A sense of purpose began to grow in her heart. Yes, she would bring back many with her to the beautiful land. That would be fantastic!

Both she and the ram had remained silent as they traversed the treacherous valley. As they entered the thick forest, the ram broke the silence. "I will be taking a different route than you tomorrow. Remember all you have learned. You are not alone. The Father's Spirit is in your heart and will teach you and comfort you. Listen to His still voice and talk often with Him. It is He who taught the desert horses. He will teach you as well. Stay focused on Him. Don't forget why you're here.

"The Darklord has many tricks. He will try to get your mind on things other than your true mission. He has no power over you. His only weapon is to deceive you. He has taken the truth and twisted it just enough to make what he says seem right. It is not what the Father intended. The Spirit within you will reveal any falseness. Let the Spirit be your friend and guide. I will check on you as often as I am able.

"Once a week, you should return to the forest. Climb to the cliffs and gaze on the beautiful land. It is good to think on where you are going and reflect on all that is good that you have learned. Listen and be still. Focus on the Father and feel His joy and strength within. This will help keep your hope alive and well.

"There is so much more I wish to share with you. Right now it would only be so many words. The Spirit will teach you all that you need to know. Some lessons will come easy; others will be quite painful. All are necessary. Trust that He loves you and will work all things together for good."

And on the morrow, they went their separate ways. She went back to the Shadowlands and shared with all that would listen about the Father's love. She told them of the beautiful land. Once a week, they would make the trek through the woods to gaze on the lands of light beyond the mists. From time to time the old ram would stop and visit. They began to notice that their own land did not seem quite so dark.

Chapter Eight

The young colt had grown into a strong and beautiful filly. The climb to the cliffs had given her great strength. She glowed with the Spirit's light. One day, as she passed the track where the strong and beautiful horses ran, the owner called out. "Come here, My Beauty."

"What?" she thought. "He couldn't possibly be talking to me!" As she looked around she saw no one else.

Again he repeated, "Come here, My Beauty."

Now, no one had ever called her beautiful before. Though she didn't really trust the owner, she did find it strangely exciting to be called beautiful. Entranced, she watched as he approached and slipped a silken cord around her neck. The stranger was speaking, "Come, My Beauty, let's see how fast you are."

Does he want me to run with the beautiful horses? Surely not! I'm just an ordinary horse. Exciting possibilities tumbled through her mind. *Surely he was mistaken. I could never be a beautiful horse, but it would be fun to run with them just this once!*

They strapped a saddle on her back and took her and some others to the starting gate. Little monkeys jumped on their backs and grabbed the reins. Several of the horses were fidgety and tense. All they had ever wanted was to win this race. They eyed each other guardedly, wondering who their competition was.

She looked at the others. They were so well groomed and had been training all their lives to race. *No, I couldn't possibly win, but it will be fun to see what I can do!*

Her muscles quivered with excitement. She focused on the track and then suddenly they were off! Quickly she stretched out into a long easy run. It felt so good to be running into the wind. Her mane and tail were flying free, her long legs reaching for the turf before her and pushing it behind. She was racing the wind and so wrapped up in the joy of the run that she hadn't even noticed the others. Suddenly she wondered where the others were. Was she all alone? Glancing back she saw them a quarter of a lap behind! It couldn't be! *I must be doing something wrong. Maybe I'm running too hard too quickly.* But it felt so good, and there was only a quarter of a lap to go. She backed off a bit into an easy lope. Maybe they were saving some of their energy because they'd have to run again, or something. Soon she crossed the finish line . . . way in front of the others. She couldn't believe it! Suddenly there were coaches and trainers everywhere planning her life!

"She'd look really good if we braided silk ribbons in her mane and tail."

"Well, I think we should cut her mane and give her a more modern look."

"I'll give her tips on how to run a real race."

"Well, I think we should train her like the southern horses. I'll train her so she can win the big race."

No one seemed to notice that she'd won the race easily by a great distance without coaching or ribbons in her mane. No one asked what she'd been doing to get so strong. No one wondered why she was so alive, joyful, and enthusiastic. They weren't really interested in the truth. This was an opportunity to exploit someone while putting themselves in the limelight. If they had been wise, they would have asked her these things. She would have told them of the weekly climbs through the strong, quiet forest and the hope in her heart as she gazed at the land where horses flew. She would have told them of her goal to share the love and joy she had found and to lead them back to the beautiful land of the flying ones.

She was bustled off to a stall and fed a rich dinner of oats and special blend of corn, wheat, and molasses. The following weeks were a blur of fancy dinners, timed workouts, and hours alone in her stall. It didn't feel natural. She missed running wild and free, and the long hard climbs through the forest to the cliffs. Surely, these coaches knew what they were doing, though. It was what they lived for.

She began to feel a deep uneasiness in the pit of her belly. There was always chatter about things that just really didn't matter. Who cared if her hoofs were black or purple? Who cared what so-and-so was wearing. Oh, how she longed for the strong quiet of the forest, the cheery birds' songs, and laughing brook.

Finally, the day of the big race arrived. She would do her best to do what the coaches had shown her. It just didn't seem to flow like it used to, but they must be right. She was concentrating so hard on what she was supposed to do these days that it just wasn't fun any more. Her heart ached to guide her. "No, she must listen to the coaches."

Her life had become one big effort to win a race. As she looked around at the other racers and listened, she became aware of the futility of it all. She overheard one horse tell another that her life would be over if she didn't win. She had trained for this all her life and her owner was going to send her back to the plowing fields if she didn't win.

Now, the really funny thing was that all of these horses were fast and beautiful, but only one could win. On any given day any one of them might win, but their future depended on only one performance. The really sad thing was that only one could win and the others would be treated like losers.

Inside, a great discontent began to rise. She was angry that so many felt so bad. Why did only one have to win? Deep in her heart she knew she was not as fast as she had been. The food they'd fed her was too rich and she'd gained weight. More than that, she now ran with her head and not her heart. The joy of the run was gone. She didn't feel wild and free. She felt cut off and trapped. Everything she did was regulated. She thought of her friends racing the wind for the joy of it! All of them raced the wind and felt joy. None of them felt sad because they weren't out in front. They went where their heart and spirit took them. There was no comparison of great or least among them. Everyone's journey was special. They rose to meet challenges and grew strong and beautiful, each in their own way.

This race stuff was sad and empty. There was no point to it other than to see who could make it around the circle first. Only one could feel joy afterwards. It wasn't real. It was a pale simulation of what was natural and an attempt to quantify it and package it. It was not truth. She was sure that none of the trained horses could catch the desert horses. They ran with their hearts and with purpose. Their lives depended on it. This was an imitation of real life. The desert horses were busy with the living of their lives. It didn't matter to them who could run in a circle the fastest. What did matter was that as a group, they escaped predators and found food and grew strong of body, soul, and spirit.

No, her life was not about running in senseless circles. She was eager to get back to her wild open places, to feel the strong quiet peace within. Suddenly, they were off! She knew what she must do. Gathering her will into a tight determined energy she dashed past the others, stretching her neck forward as far as it would reach. Her whole body seemed to stretch lower to the ground. Her feet seemed to fly. There was a sense of desperation in her run. The onlookers noticed and thought, "She must want to win more than anything in the world! She is a winner for sure."

Then . . . much to their amazement, she gathered herself and jumped the fence at the far turn. The frightened monkey leapt from her back and grabbed the fence as she sailed gracefully over. She ran over the bridge, through the city, and into the forest.

It had been a year since she had climbed to the cliffs. Oh, how her heart ached to gaze into the land beyond. Even the air smelled good. She'd forgotten the warm, woodsy smells. She was weeping and laughing all at once remembering the joy of freedom. Who cared if she could run in a circle and have ribbons in her hair? This is what she longed for. This is where she belonged. Here it didn't matter what she could do, but who she was inside. Overcome with emotion, she sobbed violently as a volley of feelings poured out of her heart.

Finally, the pain of fullness subsided. It was all poured out. Inside was a cleanness and quietness. Sweet exhaustion overtook her. Rest would not come though. Now that there was room and quiet inside, a deep sadness began to fill the void. Slowly, it began to dawn on her that for the past year she had totally forgotten her mission. Quietly, she stood as the emptiness of the past year passed through her mind's eye. Humbly, under her breath, she whispered, "Father, forgive me if you can. Please help me."

All was still. The inner emotional storm had exhausted her. From out of the still quiet depths of her heart she heard a quiet voice. "I love you, and you are forgiven. Peace and joy be with you." The words splashed a healing balm. It rippled outward through her whole being and continued into the far beyond. As it rippled, part of her heart followed it. It was as if she were one with the life and goodness around her.

Quietly now, she walked as if in a dream to the cliffs. She heard every precious birdsong and scurrying critter. She saw the silent deer and felt their heart and strength. They were her brothers. The grasses rustled amiably, and she felt their life force touch her spirit. Even the rocks gave off an aura of strength. It was as if all of creation had joined together to heal her spirit.

Finally the cliffs! Reverently, she stood and gazed at the awesome beauty of the golden desert, the rolling foothills, and the great purple mountains. Her whole being vibrated with a strong and quiet peace. Again she wept, not from pain, but at the joy of forgiveness and the realization of the Father's great love and patience.

The old ram seemed to rise out of the mists below. He joined her quiet meditation. Somehow, she knew that he knew of her faithlessness. He seemed to love and accept her anyway.

Turning, she sighed, "What happened? I truly wanted to help bring more horses here. I haven't even seen my old friends in a year. It was as if nothing else mattered except being the best circle runner."

"Hmmm," mulled the old ram. "I'm not so sure that it's particularly wrong to circle run as long as you have right priorities and motives. You are young yet and have much to learn about the Darklord's tactics and how they can be used against him."

"What do you mean? What did the Darklord have to do with any of it?"

"What were you thinking about this last year?" the old ram gently asked.

Lowering her eyes and looking away to hide her pain at the answer she must give, she slowly replied, "I was thinking about myself and how to keep the audience thinking I was beautiful and fast. I never really totally felt like I fit in. I was afraid they would think I was just ordinary and send me away or not like me. As time went on, it felt like I was only important to them because of what I could do, not because of what I was inside. All they talked about was what I did and how I looked. No one ever asked how I felt or what I thought. I don't think they really cared."

"Would it surprise you if I told you that everyone there felt just like you did? They were just as afraid to talk as you were. The Darklord started the lie. He convinced them that it only matters what you look like and what you can do. They've been playing the game so long that they don't know that life can be better. Most go home at night with an empty feeling in the pit of their stomach. They feel cold, alone, and afraid. Afraid that tomorrow someone may see through the charade to what they really are inside and reject them.

"It only takes a few brave souls to speak up and not be afraid. Misery is their prison, and fear and silence are the locks that keep them there.

"When the owner first saw you, it was his intent to turn you away from your personal mission and replace it with another goal. Had you been wiser in such things, you could have told them what made you swift and strong and taught them. You could have challenged their ways and had them test their methods against yours.

"They all wanted to be a part of what they saw in you. They did it the only way they knew how. Instead of you sharing your secret so they could be like you, they pulled you into their own misery. Even there was an opportunity. You could have shared openly of the emptiness and misery you felt. All of them would have identified and known exactly what you were talking about. You could have shared with them about the beautiful land where they could run wild and free, and of the love and forgiveness the Father has for them. Not all would have followed, but many would have. Some would have been afraid of change and clung tenaciously to their charades. However, you would have planted a seed of hope in them that there was more than the *game* to life. They would begin to hope that someone might love them for who they are inside and that they might find something to fill the big emptiness."

The horse sadly hung her head. Her heart ached for the others in misery. Great tears splashed from her eyes to the ground.

"Child, I did not share these things to sadden you, only to open your eyes to possibilities. The Father works all things together for good. He knows you're not perfect and may be easily tricked. Wisdom comes with age. It takes time. Learn to listen to your heart. The voice of His Spirit will speak to your heart and your very depths."

"What good can come of my running away when I should have helped the others?" she asked balefully.

"You did the best you could. You broke free! You could have won the race but chose to flee. Now, every single one of them is wondering why you gave up the thing they covet and live for. They don't understand and are troubled. Many aren't sure why you left, but will receive courage to begin their own journey because of your courageous act. They have grown weary and sick of the game. Deep inside they want more. When they seek, they will find."

Night fell peacefully around them. She had learned much and had many things to contemplate. Right now she was exhausted. Tomorrow was another beginning.

Chapter Nine

Warm fingers of light reached over the mountains to waken her. Slowly, she stretched in response to its tender touch and the stirrings around her. She saw the old ram making preparations to leave.

"I'm going to the desert. Would you like to come?" He queried.

"No, I think I just want to rest for awhile," she replied.

"Very well," said the ram. "I'll see you later."

She watched as he disappeared into the white mists. Her heart tugged to go after him, but she'd made up her mind. She was just going to rest for awhile. "Besides," she reasoned to herself, "it's hard work to go on a journey, and I've earned a break."

As the day progressed, she wandered aimlessly eating grasses, napping, and looking at all of the beauty around her. She felt the quiet soaking into her. Day after day went by, each like the one before it. It was as if she existed in a quiet, never-ending dreamland. There was no past; there was no future. She was in the state of *just being*.

One morning, new sounds rippled through the air, dispelling the outer quiet but not touching the peace that had grown strong within her. Snorting, laughter, and the thud of running hoofs drew nearer and nearer. Quietly, she took a concealed position behind a bush and watched to see what would unfold. Suddenly, pounding hoofs and flying manes and tails flashed past her. Their thundering rhythm was so contagious that without thinking she found herself racing after them and thoroughly enjoying the group run. She tossed her head and flared her nostrils wide to capture the rushing winds and the scent of the others. Oh, what a glorious run! As they neared the cliffs their hoofs dug in and they skidded to a halt.

Glancing around, she noticed several familiar faces. These were her friends! It had been a year since she'd seen them. They recognized her too!

"Where have you been? We thought you'd disappeared forever!"

She scuffed the ground with her hoof and looked off into the distance. Searching deep, she sought for something to say that wouldn't expose the delicate fibers of heart and mind that was still weaving her healing. Any lack of sensitivity on their part might tear the fine healing gauze that was not yet complete. She drew her focus back to their expectant faces, noting their genuine concern. Perhaps she owed them some explanation.

Hesitantly she spoke. "I was a circle runner this past year."

Now they looked at her in awe. "Wow," they echoed in hushed tones. "Are you still running?" they asked with curiosity.

"No," she said bluntly, wishing to avoid any further delving into the past year's events. "It's not all it's cracked up to be. Parts of it were fun and interesting, but mostly it was so empty and shallow. Now, if you don't mind, I'd much rather hear about you."

They looked at her in disbelief. How could anyone not love being a circle runner with all the attention and glory? Still, she was their friend and they honored her request.

With a sigh of relief, she changed the subject. "So what have you guys been up to?" Looking around she saw several unfamiliar faces.

"Well, we've been coming up here once a week and thinking about the flying horses. Some of us have been recruiting others to join us. One of the older mares remembers the ancient stories and has been telling them to us. It would be great if you would join us again. I bet we could get more to come hear about the flying horses if you would tell them that you were a circle runner. They'll respect that."

"Maybe that would be OK," she answered.

She decided to rejoin the faithful group. They sang and prayed and told all who would listen, that the Creator loved them and forgave them and wanted them to follow Him. She kind of hedged the issue of flying, because in actuality she had never flown or really known anyone who had. They were a diligent group. Often they grew weary. It seemed the more they spoke of love and forgiveness, the more they saw misery and sadness around them, even in their own ranks.

She joined a particularly diligent horse to start a family with. Now, the male horse wanted to follow the ancient teaching and have a good family and serve the Creator. It worried him that something might happen to her or that she might leave him, so he made her stay in a corral while he went and told others about love and forgiveness.

"May I go and study with the Old Ones, or go into the country while you are gone?" she asked.

"No, something might happen to you. I'll teach you what you need to know and take you where you need to go. I'm in charge, and I want you in the corral."

Days turned into months, and she felt so alone. *Was this what it was all about? Had she left her mother's dusty corral for this?* Her heart began to search. She cried out to the Father, and her heart was comforted, but her misery continued.

Then one day she was blessed with a son. All of her energies were poured into this young colt. Now her days were full, and her heart was satisfied because of the young one.

Her male had heard of a place that taught the ancient stories, but it took twinkly rocks to go. "They get twinkly rocks near my mother's corral," she offered.

"Good. You can stay near your mother while I get twinkly rocks for school. This will help me be better at telling people about the love," the male reasoned.

So they moved back to where she started. It was good to see her mother again. She told her of the lush grasses, clear waters, and warm sunshine. They spoke of many things, but not all. Her male went deep into the hills so he could get lots of twinkly rocks. He was gone for weeks at a time. Her son enjoyed playing with the grandmother in her corral.

One day, she had an idea and spoke of it to the grandmother. "I am young and strong. I think I should go to the nearby fields and help earn twinkly rocks while you are watching our son. Are you willing to do this for me?"

The grandmother was delighted and replied with a loving smile. "I would love to watch your son. We'll be just fine."

"Are you sure? I don't want to be a burden, but it just seems that I should be doing something to help out."

"You run along now," her mother replied. "We'll be just fine."

Ahh! An adventure at last! It felt so good to be going somewhere that she could be around other horses her own age. No more dusty corral for her!

At first, the work was hard. She hadn't exercised in oh, so long. Eventually, her muscles grew strong and she felt so alive and happy. She was a good worker and was elated to have comradeship again! Something else was happening too. The work foreman found out that she had been a circle runner and began to address her as though she were special. Her heart went out to him with such intensity that it frightened her. It felt wonderful and scary all at once. She loved going to work now for two reasons. It felt good to have her efforts appreciated and it felt good to be noticed by the dark, handsome foreman.

Once, when he passed her he spoke under his breath. "Why do you have to be married?" How her heart ached. How she longed to walk away from her dusty corral with her son and go with him. How she longed to declare her love for him. He had gone out on a limb to declare himself to her, and she had remained silent. She was so afraid that he might see in her eyes the intensity of what she felt for him that she lowered her eyes and walked away. Her heart was deep in anguish at the hurt she was causing him by not responding.

That night, after her son fell asleep, she cried until she thought her heart would break. This was so hard. Her male was so wrapped up in his own life that she didn't feel she even mattered to him. Here was one who she cared for that cared back. It just wasn't fair! But she would do what was right. She wouldn't go against the ancient teachings, even though two hearts were breaking. She felt like a martyr.

The next day, the foreman announced he was going away. Later, he spoke to her alone. "You think I'm horrible, don't you?" he asked her directly.

"No," she said faltering. Fighting valiantly to maintain her composure and stay true to her own male. "I think you're great, and I've enjoyed working with you. I hope all goes well with you." And with that, she turned and walked away while her heart fell to pieces; each piece taking wing and flying to the one she loved.

Her heart was gone. With stoic resolve, she went back to her own dusty corral, but her heart and mind followed the one she loved. Part of her felt guilty and part of her no longer cared.

Now when the group went to the mountain to search the horizon for the flying horses, she was silent. She knew it was wrong to think of the other male, but she couldn't stop herself. Who could she ask for help without breaking the heart of her own male or revealing to the others the mess she was inside? Truly, she had become a wretched miserable creature. Finally, she talked to the Father and asked forgiveness and for another child to help her forget the foreman she loved.

Again she was blessed, this time with a daughter. The little one was sweet and beautiful and gave her great joy. The son was so helpful and loving. Together, they filled her days with love and sweetness. The poor little daughter had colic the first few months and kept her up all night. During the day she tended to her son. Eventually, it took its toll on her energies. Now she was physically and emotionally drained and began to dream again of the one she loved. Her male, however, was more intent than ever on his quest to become a teacher of love and was oblivious to her tattered heart and spirit. Once, she almost bolted and ran when the gate to the corral was ajar. But she loved her two young ones and forced herself to stay.

Like the walking dead, she went through the motions of life. Her heart was gone; her spirit almost snuffed out. One morning, she woke and couldn't move. Frightened, she struggled, but to no avail. Slowly she rolled her eyes to see why she couldn't move. Massive chains were wrapped around her. She strained to see the desert. Deep inside, she felt as though she would surely die. Quickly now, the pieces of her heart returned. They were flying to her aide, for she was in great need of love and care. As her heart grew stronger, so did the pain, as it began to knit itself back together. But with the pain, came the desire to live and be free. In an effort to live, she screamed out to the Father for help.

The old ram appeared and sadly spoke. "Child, why have you suffered so long?"

Dropping her eyes she whispered, "I was so ashamed. I kept thinking if I just tried harder, if I'd ask forgiveness and really try, that I'd get it taken care of. Now I don't know what's going on at all. I really need your help."

Tenderly the old ram looked at her. With great kindness he asked, "And what was going on before?"

Mournfully, she looked at him, her heart in her eyes. "I cared about another. I think I took care of it," she said painfully. "What I need help with now is these chains. If I don't get free, I will die. How did they get here?"

Sadly, the old ram whispered "You put them there."

Startled, she threw her head back searching his eyes for answers. "How?"

Gently he spoke "It is all the anger inside your heart."

"I have no anger in my heart!" she replied indignantly.

"Hmmm," mulled the old ram. "Why did you stay in this old dusty corral all these years? Why weren't you doing what was in your heart? Have you found your wings?"

Suddenly, she was saturated with anger. I married someone that I thought was serving the Father. Yes, I'm angry that he hid me away and did what he wanted while I was dying inside. But according to the old teachings, he said I was supposed to submit to him or I wouldn't please the Father."

"Child, words can be twisted and misunderstood by selfish people in order to control others. Always trust the Father's voice and heart above all. The Father said for each to submit to the other and for the male to love the female the same as the Son loved us all. The Son died so we could be with Him forever."

"Now, look within your heart and name your chains and know that it is not wrong to be angry at injustice. It is wrong to hang onto the anger. Then, once you feel it, forgive the source and hand that chain to the Father."

Kindly, the ram knelt down and kissed her forehead. Ever so softly he whispered in her ear. "This is wisdom from the Son. Think on it and live. He says, 'I desire mercy, not sacrifice.'"

As she gazed into his loving eyes, a gossamer strand of light wafted its way deep within her and wound tenderly around her heart weaving a safe cocoon for the release of pain and anger. She felt a strange peace and resolve flower within. She knew full well the brutal task that lay before her. Her heart trembled wretchedly, and for the first time in a long time, her mind allowed the painful messages from the heart to be heard. Old messages long buried now rose unbidden, urgently seeking aide for the heart so long in crisis. Cries of pain, long silent, now found release.

Her mind, formerly unwilling to share the heart's pain, now recoiled at the intensity and volume of hurts raging forth in torrents. Suddenly, the floodgates were closed. She could bear no more this day. As she viewed the memories that had surfaced, tears poured from her heart. The gossamer cocoon of light, now crimson from the heart's pains, held the tattered heart oh, so softly, keeping the spirit within alive and bound safely to the body. Had it not been there, the spirit may have despaired and flown away. As the tears washed away the pain, her mind became angry that the tender heart had born so much. And the anger was alive and grew as large as the pain it had replaced. "Aaauuugh!" she cried as she tossed her head, wishing to somehow right the wrong.

Softly, the ram whispered again. "Forgive, Child, forgive. That is your only release. Give the anger to God and He will bring justice where it is needed."

"It is hard to let go!" she raged. "I want to hurt what has hurt me! It is so unfair!"

"I know, Child, but there are things you do not understand. What twisted pain in that other soul gave rise to its own misery?"

"Aaauuugh!" she screamed as the anger consumed her.

"Let it go, Child, or the anger will weave its own terrible web, keeping you forever in its grasp. Break free. Reach deep in your heart and mind, and wrench it up by the roots! Give the whole thing into the Father's care. Forgive the offender, and you will be free."

With great determination she spoke. "Father, I choose to forgive. Take this pain and anger from me. Let your love flow through me to those I meet."

Exhausted, she slept. The ram watched over her through the night. On the morrow, she noticed some of the chains had disappeared, but not all. "I feel better," she spoke thankfully to her old friend.

"I will stay by your side and comfort your heart as it sheds its pain."

"Thank you, Friend."

In the days that followed, the ram gave her nourishment and water. He stayed close by as her heart continued to pour out its pain. It became easier to give the anger away and to love and forgive the offender. She had learned to anticipate the growing lightness and cleanness that was slowly replacing the heavy chains. Finally, the last chain was shed. She felt so free and light!

She stood unshackled and looked longingly to the desert. Her heart began to race and thoughts of running free became overwhelming. It was as if freedom from her chains allowed her heart to beat to a new rhythm. It beat stronger and stronger until she could hear nothing but its beat pounding and singing in her whole being.

That night as she slept, she dreamed she was running beside a beautiful moonlit ocean. The water was moon kissed with sparkles of light. The trees even had leaves of silver. As she ran, she noticed the most magnificent swan flying right beside her. The two journeyed side by side for a time. Then, an amazing thing happened. The swan moved closer and closer till he actually merged with her. Only the swan's wings now showed as he continued to fly through her. She was no longer running, but airborne, flying among the stars!!! She felt so glorious and free!

The next morning she awoke with the freedom of the dream wrapped around her. She didn't understand what it meant, but she knew it had something to do with the other flying horses. She looked tenderly at her two young colts. They were well fed and cared for. Their father would watch over them. She became frightened at what she was thinking of doing, but she also felt a growing excitement. She knew she must do this thing . . . to go to the desert to seek the flying horses! She would do this thing and come find her colts and show them the way!

Chapter Ten

Three years had passed. She stood alone on the cliff overlooking the misty valley. Far away she could see the rugged desert and majestic mountains. Great tears rolled down her cheeks. "What have I done?" she asked quietly to no one in particular. "This isn't what I wanted. I just wish everything would vanish, and I could start over. Now I'll never get it right."

Her head hung low, and her eyes closed tightly. It was painful to think of her old hopes and dreams. "I really wanted to be a flying horse," she cried. "Now I'll never make it."

A deep familiar voice rose from the mists. "Little One, are you there?"

Shame washed through her in waves. She wanted to run and hide. How could she face her old friend and teacher? Softly she spoke half hoping she wouldn't be heard.

Maybe he would just keep going and let her disappear into the shadows. "I'm here."

The old ram appeared out of the mists and stopped right beside her.

"How have you been, My Child?" he asked tenderly.

She began to shake violently as the pain in her heart broke free. Broken dreams and plans, shame and heartaches came rushing to the surface, tumbling over each other, cascading forth in great tears.

When she had finally quieted the outburst, the old ram asked, "Have you been sharing the Father's love with others?"

Again, troubled waters rose from her heart to her sad eyes. "I can't," she sobbed.

"Why not?" the old ram asked kindly.

"I am so unworthy." she whispered sadly. "I've made such a mess of my life. No one would ever want to listen to me. What have I got to share with others that will help them when I can't even get my own life right?"

"Child, why are you here at the cliffs?"

"I don't know. I guess I was hoping for some miracle to make everything better. All I saw was where I never went, and I remembered the dreams of flying that will never be."

"Child, you are closer to flying than you've ever been."

"What?" she asked. Her eyes opened wide in disbelief. A muffled sob trembled through her and caught in her throat.

"Do you remember your search for the secret of dust?"

"Yes."

"Well, the search for your wings to fly is not unlike that search. True, you have chosen a painful path for your search, but . . . the Father can work all things together for our good. He will not hide his truth from those who seek Him with their whole heart."

"Do you mean that there's still a chance I might become a flying horse? You don't know how badly I've messed up." She lowered her eyes in deep despair.

"Do you love the Father's Son?"

"Yes."

"If I told you there was a way for everything to turn out right, would you be willing to go that way . . . no matter what?"

Quietly and with returning resolve and hope, she replied, "Tell me the way."

"High in the mountains, there is a house of stone and light that was built many years ago by those who sought the Truth. In the center of this, there is a small lake. It is the Lake of Truth, and its waters are powerful. Most cannot bear the whole truth and they stop short of their quest. If you seek with your whole heart to know the truth, the truth will set you free. The waters are alive."

"In the morning and evening when you have drunk deeply, then gaze into the water and see what you see. Do not turn away, but speak the truth that is revealed. On the third day, if you desire the Truth with your whole heart, you will find what you seek."

"I will go and do this thing. I cannot continue in the way I am going or I will surely die. I am so miserable."

"Do not lose heart. It is the spirit within that causes the misery and seeks to draw you to the truth and the Father's loving arms. He wants good things for you, but you must follow Him and obey Him."

"I will go, though I fear this journey. I've made some really horrible mistakes. Right now, I'd just be glad if he'd let me serve those who serve Him. That at least would be something closer to Him."

"Godspeed, Child. Stay on the narrow path. Seek the truth and remember He loves you. His Spirit will guide you."

Slowly, she walked away down into the mists. This was her first time to venture into the mists without the ram. "Spirit, guide me safely through," she whispered. Her eyes were glued to the path. As she placed each foot forward, she could see only far enough to place the next foot. With repetition, she began to relax and found herself once again humming the old ram's song. It felt good to be on her quest again. No longer was the quest born out of enthusiasm and good intentions but out of stolid resolve tempered by the knowledge of her own shortcomings. She was determined to see this through and end her current misery.

Her heart, mind, and body were keenly focused on listening, seeing, and hearing where the Spirit led. The song she sang rose from the spirit within and comforted and encouraged her.

Then, there was the desert. She did not stop, but walked silently into its vastness. Soon, she felt at one with the shifting sands and soft winds. Her own thoughts shifted and tumbled and moved in the winds. Memories of the past played silently before her mind's eye. It was as if she were viewing someone else's life from afar. It was a strange feeling. Quiet contemplation was all that she felt as her life ran through her mind.

The mountains loomed before her shrouded in mist. She began the treacherous climb with no thought of possible dangers. A quest, finally a quest! She had regained her hope of finding her own wings. Nothing else mattered. The clouds burst open and drenched her with their waters, washing away the desert dust and purifying the air. The fresh scent of wild flowers wafted by. She could almost taste them in the swirling winds. A bright rainbow touched the earth. Rays of sun broke through the dark storm clouds warming her. The air grew crisp and cool as she climbed higher and higher. Its cold was sharp and bit her lungs but she found the pure sweetness of it very pleasant.

Scraggly trees, worn and twisted by the mountain storms, clung resolutely to their rocks like stalwart sentinels. They weren't tall, or perfect, or pretty, but a strong, rugged beauty radiated from them. They were trees you could count on. Nothing could shake them from their perch. Their roots were sunk deep in the rock of the mountain.

Before her lay a quiet meadow nestled in a hidden hollow of the mountainside. Flowers swayed gently in the breeze and danced gaily to the delicate symphony of twittering birds, rustling grasses, creaking trees, and the gurgling brook. A small deer leapt daintily over the sparkling brook and peered shyly at her. Then, with a single bound, it vanished. Droning bees, laden with sweet treasure from the fragrant flowers, flew slowly collecting more of the sweetness. Suddenly, all grew quiet; the hush fell heavy on her ear.

The storm rose quickly, once again hiding the sun. All had vanished. Again, she pressed upward through sharp steep rocks. Lightning cracked nearby with great force. The fury of the storm felt good and strong as it whipped and lashed her mane and tail in its gusty onslaughts. Her nostrils flared as she felt its power permeate and become part of her being. She felt so strong and alive! The winds raged stronger and stronger lifting her spirit high. An eagle soared high in the raging winds. His powerful wings were spread taut. The wind currents pushed him higher and higher till he vanished from sight!

Resolutely, she turned her face back to the path she must take. "I too will be aided by the winds to reach my goal." she said with renewed determination. Feeling inspired and encouraged, she quickened her pace, which resulted in several cuts and bruises from the jagged, unyielding rocks. From time to time, the clouds would part, and she would see glimpses of the path and peak before her.

Night came. All was still and dark. Wearily, she rested on a grassy outcrop, oblivious to the elements while her mind dreamed of soaring to the top of the mountain. The next morning as she woke, nothing was visible but a thick fog. She had seen glimpses of where she must go and began to feel her way slowly up the path, one step at a time. Not seeing clearly was very discouraging and frustrating.

"I hope I'm on the right path. Please guide me." she whispered to the Spirit. Deep inside, she knew that she was indeed moving upward, for each step was more difficult than the last. The air was growing cooler. Soon all that seemed to exist was her exhaustion. The only thing that seemed to change was the movement of her feet. Time was nonexistent. Her emotions vanished; she felt nothing, only movement, seemingly without purpose. No longer did she dream of the beautiful heights. There was only difficult motion.

The fog continued for days. At night, she dreamed only of fog.

During the day, she saw the fog and felt only the fatigue of her own difficult climb into it. The only difference between night and day was difficult movement. Her movement began to seem meaningless. She grew weary.

"Why am I doing this?" she questioned dully.

As she spoke, she became aware of the emotional pain and turmoil within her. She could see or feel nothing but her own heart and mind. The misery and pain of the past few years ached within. She wanted to do anything but look inside. Oh, how she cringed as she thought of deeds and words she wished to recall. Her spirit groaned within at the load it bore up the mountain. As she groaned and toiled upward, the dream she'd had long ago of flying among the stars came to ease her pain. With that memory came a spark of hope. She began to remember why she was on this quest. Thinking of the possibility of flying fanned the spark of hope to a small flame. Resolve to reach her destination returned.

Perhaps it was the flame in her heart that melted away the dreary fog. She began to notice that the higher she climbed the less dense the fog was. It was growing lighter as she made upward progress. The next morning the sun shone cheerily on the mountains. With great astonishment, she saw the lake and house of stone and light before her!

"Yes! I made it! Oh, thank you, Spirit, for getting me here," she shouted fervently.

As she turned and looked down the trail she gasped in a husky whisper, "Wow!" Before her lay the most awesome panorama she had ever seen. Off in the distance she saw the dark mists of the Shadowlands rolling to meet the white mists that shrouded the narrow path. She saw the great golden desert with its splendid mesas and hidden canyons. She could see beyond her own mountain, to many others and to a vast sea of water she'd never even heard of. Oh, there was so much more than she had ever imagined! With deep emotion, she saw the path that she had recently navigated.

"I can't believe I actually made it." She wept in sweet relief.

Slowly, she turned towards her destination. The large stone structure was toppled and crumbling. It didn't look so very special or impressive. A deep disappointment rose within her. She wasn't sure what she'd been expecting. The structure was in great disrepair. No one seemed to come here or care that it was crumbling. She had hoped for some great revelation.

Ah well, the lake was still there. It was smooth as glass. As she approached to drink the still waters, a great uneasiness came over her. What would these waters reveal? She drank deeply. Oh, it tasted so good! Having drunk her fill, she looked into the waters as she had been told.

She saw herself so clearly . . . not only herself. Her colts were there. She saw them in the distance. They were sad and crying for her. Her heart froze in horror. No longer did she see her own reflection up close but in the distance. Again she froze, almost in shock as she saw herself dancing in the neon houses and looking for male companionship.

"Aaauuugh!" she groaned as her heart wrenched in pain. "What was I thinking? What was I doing?" she anguished. "Oh my poor babies, my poor babies . . . . I am so sorry. I am so sorry." Finally, the pain her children had borne had become her own. It ripped and tore through her heart with great wrenching sobs. Her body shuddered violently as the pain exceeded her very being and fell to the ground in great pools. She wept and anguished until she could feel no more. Exhausted, she slept, though not a peaceful sleep. Visions of her children alone and full of sorrow haunted her dreams, and her heart grieved even as she slept.

The coolness of the approaching night restored her to consciousness. She felt no hunger, only deep, deep sorrow as she approached the pool to drink. Sorrow and humility now governed her movements. She closed her eyes with resolve and lowered her mouth to draw in the clear waters. Slowly and with great deliberation she opened her eyes. Again she saw herself, and then far away she saw herself with one of her boyfriends and then another and another and another. In the distance she saw her first husband weeping in pain. A dagger pierced her heart as she felt his misery at her own unfaithfulness. "I'm so sorry. I'm so sorry," she wept. "I was so miserable myself, I only thought of my own pain. You trusted me to be your wife forever, and I left." She wept till exhaustion overtook her. Again, she slept a restless, grieving sleep.

Sunlight warmed her to consciousness. With great determination she drank again, though she had only found great pain from doing so. Reluctantly, she peered at the mirror before her, cringing in expectation. This time she saw her second husband. He was being so kind, teaching her and allowing her to grow and learn. Sadly she saw herself demanding his attention, restricting his freedom, and accusing him of not loving her. Oh, how she cringed at her own wretched, hurtful words. She wept at having driven his sweet caring Spirit from her. Again she slept wearily.

At sunset she rose and sorrowfully approached the waters and drank again. Woefully and with great hesitation she opened her eyes. Her many boyfriends appeared again, now following their own way, not the Father's way. A horrible truth dawned on her. In horror, she realized she had not shared the Father's love with them! "Aaauuugh! Oh Father!" she wept. "Send worthy messengers to share your love for them. I have failed them miserably. Do not allow them to go to hell because I forgot my mission. Send others more worthy who will share your great love and truth with them." And she wept for those she had failed and wounded.

Morning came. This was the third day. Tonight the truth she sought would be revealed. She dreaded the waters and the painful things they might reveal about her own self. Yet, strangely, there was a relief at finally seeing the truth. She used to explain and reason away any wrong doing on her part. Now she saw the truth revealed, her own rottenness burst before her like a rupturing boil—painful, and less painful, all at once.

Quietly and soberly she drank the still waters. Again her children appeared before her, but this time they were grown. She saw them struggling in relationships of their own. The pain she had caused them and her absence from their lives and her own wretched example had given them a painful legacy. They now struggled with the same issues she had battled and lost. What sad inheritance she had bestowed on her offspring.

"Aaauuugh!" she groaned. "I wish I had persevered and overcome the difficult situations instead of giving in to my own willfulness and selfish desires." Dejectedly she wept at the trials her children now faced.

This was all so unbearable. With great resolve she spoke. "This time I shall persevere to the end and be done with it. If I perish, I perish. I have sinned terribly against my children, my husbands, my friends, and myself. What else is there to reveal?"

Silently she waited. For the first time she saw herself the way others had seen her. No longer could she hide behind her own explanations of her behaviors. The truth was horrifying. Surely the old ram must've been mistaken when he'd said that she was close to finding her wings. He didn't know all of this. Still she waited alone with her thoughts.

Finally evening arrived. With dread and hope she drank the last drink. A vast mass of horses turned to look at her with a sad, wistful, soul hunger in their eyes. Sadly they turned from her with eyes now vacant and walked into a dark abyss!

"Oh Father, I didn't know so many were waiting to hear! I have failed so miserably. I should have been living a life that would point them to you! I should have told them about you! I am so totally selfish and thoughtless! What a miserable, wretched, selfish creature I have become! Please forgive me. Please forgive me! Please help me! Take over my life," she sobbed over and over again.

Sadly, with tear-filled eyes she gazed on her own reflection, as if for the first time. Out of the stillness came a tender voice. "Child, have you been sharing my love with others?"

She struggled to answer as her aching heart rose to her throat and great tears of remorse splashed into the lake before her. In a bare whisper she answered, "No."

"Why not?" He asked tenderly and patiently.

Then, the floodgates broke loose! Violent sobs shook her from the core to her feet. "I'm not worthy. I've made such a mess of my life, and I knew what was right! No one would believe anything I have to say."

Tenderly and with great kindness, the voice spoke comforting words. "Child, it has never been about your worthiness, but my love for you. It is my Son's goodness and love I see when I look on you. Now go and share of my love with all humility and compassion. Tell them I love them just like I love you. Tell them I forgive them just like I forgive you."

She opened her eyes in heartfelt gratefulness, and in the water before her she saw a great winged horse! She wept at its beauty and the beauty and light she felt within at the Father's love and forgiveness. As the tears cleared, she looked more closely at the lovely winged reflection before her. Startled, she realized it was herself! In great wonder and with deep emotion she spoke. "Where did the wings come from?"

"From the day you decided to follow me they have always been inside you. It takes time to grow and transform. At first you tried to do everything yourself. You tried to be what you thought I wanted you to be. You got so sidetracked and confused. Finally you were ready to give up and spoke the truth of your own shortcomings and asked me to take over. It was then that my power could be released in you. When you quit struggling to run . . . only then can I fly in you. You have to give up to me so I can take over."

That day she flew, joyfully and humbly. She felt the sweetness of life and the lightness that comes from burdens and guilt being removed. Finally she had found the secret of the flying horses! Finally, she had found her own wings! In the evening, she flew among the stars in the light of the moon, just like her dream!

Chapter Eleven

The next morning she woke with a quiet sense of joy permeating her whole being. All heaviness was gone from her heart. Only lightness and wonder remained. Even standing still, she felt as if she were floating just above the earth. Slowly she walked, radiating the joy and peace she felt inside. It seemed she had her own little world around her full of light and love. Where she walked the bubble of light and love went also.

Her old friend and mentor appeared from behind the temple ruins. With great joy she bounded towards him, cavorting in joyous circles. "I found my wings. I found my wings! I can fly!" she cried excitedly over and over. "When I thought I would surely die, I found that I could fly! He loves me!! I am forgiven!! I love Him so, sooo much!"

Then she realized that the old ram was not alone. Nearby, a small band of horses waited. They were strong and rangy looking. Though they were not pretty, they were the most beautiful and magnificent horses she had ever seen. The horses were fierce though gentle, proud yet humble, gracefully dignified yet dangerously strong and controlled all at once. Suddenly she noticed that they too had wings! Her joy was increased! Finally, the desert horses she had longed to find!

She noticed that the others were very solemn and determined looking. Their seriousness, though it quieted her jubilance, was not heavy. One of the horses walked towards her. His raven black coat glistened in the sun as he walked. Blue-black lights danced off his muscular coat. Warily, he studied her. Following close behind him were the others—pintos, chestnuts, palominos, a whole rainbow of horses!

"It is time for us to go to the Shadowlands. We have heard of the growing darkness and a horrible plan to trap the others forever in the dungeons of the Darklord. If we do not go, they will never find their wings. They will be his slaves forever. We are gathering an army of messengers to carry the light of truth into the darkness. It won't be easy. Our lives will be in danger. Will you go with us?"

"Yes." she said determinedly.

"Good. We shall need to discuss our plans and the strategy and tricks of the Darklord so that we are aware of the dangers and deceits we are up against."

The old ram interrupted. "Before we discuss this, I want to show her something which will help her understand better what we are talking about." With that, he turned to her and summoned her to follow. "Come with me, Child."

Together, the two friends walked to a breathtaking viewpoint. As she gazed at the magnificent scenery, she noticed that the white mists were gone. The narrow path surrounded by pitfalls and formerly hidden dangers appeared quite clearly now. Puzzled, she turned to the old ram. "Where did the mists go?" she asked.

"It is now, as it always was," stated the ram.

"But I don't see them now. How can it be?"

The old ram tilted his head in thought. "Let's see, how can I make this clear to you? Do you remember our first journey through the mists, and wondering how I could see where to go? Do you remember that conversation?"

"Well, sort of," she replied. "I remember something about understanding and different dimensions and two ways of looking at things. It has something to do with looking with my inner eyes at things that are real in the spiritual world, doesn't it?"

"Yes, Little One. It has to do with looking with your heart and spirit. It has to do with what is truly real and everlasting and what is temporary. It has to do with your new understanding of who you are and who the Father is. It is His Spirit unleashed in you that allowed you to see the wings He had given you. The horses with wings that you have just met are the same ones you saw running on one of our journeys. Do you remember that you saw no wings on them then?" She nodded her head. "Do you know that even if you had seen them up close, you still would not have seen their wings?"

"Why not?" she asked.

"For the same reason you could not see through the mists. Your understanding and sight was limited to the physical dimension and the here and now. The eyes of the heart and spirit can see what was; what is, and what will be. When we look at someone or some situation, we see from whence it came and the possibilities for the future."

"Do you remember your little striped friend who was going to fly?"

"Yes! What ever happened to him?" she asked.

"See that flower over there with the beautiful butterfly on it? Now look more closely. Tell me what you see."

She walked over to inspect the delicate creature more closely. Its eyes seemed somehow familiar. The butterfly began to speak. "Well hello, Friend. I see you, too, have found your wings. Were they in your heart as we thought?"

Startled at the familiar voice, she squinted and looked more closely. "Are you my little striped caterpillar friend?"

"Yes! I told you I would fly on beautiful adventures! Isn't this grand! We can both fly now!"

The old ram smiled at the two friends as they marveled how each other had changed. Finally, he interrupted their happy reunion. "The thing that I need you to understand as we prepare to go back to the Shadowlands is that those you will be speaking to do not have the same kind of sight that you now have. You need to remember back to your own days in the Shadowlands and how dark and dreary and hopeless it all seemed. Remember the things that you did not know existed, and the things you could not see. Don't be surprised that the things you share are laughed at and made fun of by those whose sight is limited. Be patient with them and continue to love them even as the Father is patient and loves you."

"I will try to remember and share His love with compassion and simplicity so that even the little ones will understand."

They rejoined the band of horses. The dark leader began to speak. "We hear that few of the horses in the Shadowlands are aware of the traps they're already in. Many drink the waters of forgetfulness or smoke the nothingness weeds. Some are burdened down with riches and toys, others with fame. There are those that can't survive in the wild because they have grown so dependent on the Darklord's jobs and way of life."

The ram interrupted. "There is a great judgment coming and all must fly to the hills and the wilds to survive. We must put aside stores of grain and have good water springs sheltered from the coming disasters."

The old ram's countenance became quite sad as he continued. "I fear that those drinking the forgetful waters will hide in them and be destroyed along with those smoking the nothingness. They won't even think of the possibility of stopping what they are doing. They have no desire to fly. They like their non-existence. They stumble through their lives in a stupor.

"Those who have accumulated so many things will stay to defend their treasures and lose their own lives. They have not yet learned to value their life and the lives of others above the things that they surround themselves with. They must give away their treasures to help others, or they will never fly to safety when they must.

"Those who glory in their own accomplishments will not want to leave that which gives them fame. They must learn to value their own heart and the hearts of others apart from their accomplishments. They must see the beauty and worth of even the humblest being.

"Those stuck in the rut of depending on others must wake up to the possibilities of change and providing for themselves. Instead of mindlessly going through the motions of living, they need to become aware of the needs of others around them and become givers instead of takers.

"Group will rise up against group and seek to destroy each other over their differences. They will desire to take from each other. The story boxes have been programming them to accept violence and evil and to mindlessly follow the crowd.

"What we now must show them is that it is better to love each other and value their differences. They must learn to share their treasures so all are fed and cared for. They must look beyond themselves and their own wants to make sure everyone's needs are met. Instead of killing each other, they must feed each other and cooperate to bring good things to all. Instead of seeking personal fame and fortune, they need to seek harmony and joy for all. They must seek to end the oppression and enslavement by the Darklord. They must turn to the Father and follow His ways."

The Ram continued his exhortation. "If they learn the truth and act on it, they will become free."

"What is the truth?"

"That the Father loves them all and wants them to love and follow Him and love each other. If they do this, the Darklord loses his power over them. The Darklord's only power is to have them remain selfish and hate and destroy each other. He doesn't want them to find their wings and fly. It's his big, cruel joke. He has them convinced they must take and hoard to be happy. In truth, only giving and sharing brings the happiness they seek. If they love the Father and forgive each other and share and love each other, the darkness will disappear and all will have joy and peace and all will prosper. The wars will end. The sadness and hopelessness will end. The hunger and abuse will end."

"But how can we few make these changes come to pass?"

"You must go throughout all the lands and speak these truths and live them. You must go in love with humility and compassion. You must be kind and patient."

"The Darklord's servants will seek to destroy you. He will escalate his own efforts to keep their minds numb and brainwashed by the story boxes. If he can keep them mindlessly watching garbage on the story box, they won't even notice the dungeons that are being built to house them forever. They'll think that the dungeons are for the lawbreakers. They will build many, and then one day, it will be too late. The Darklord's forces will round them all up and put them in the prison camps forever."

"But don't any of them know that there can't possibly be that many criminals?"

"The Darklord creates the criminals himself. They steal in order to have tokens to take the stupor pills and to buy power drugs and forgetful waters and smoke of nothingness. The greed of wanting things causes them to steal from each other. Their lack of tolerance of differences causes them to kill. Those who are in ruts just let it keep happening and do nothing until it hurts them. Then, they lash out in hate and anger and the dark circle grows larger. Their harshness is increasing and spreading so quickly now.

"You must tell them to feed their enemies who are starving and make friends of them. They must send water to the thirsty, bind up the wounds of the hurting, and take care of the widows and orphans and homeless. They need to provide schools for the ignorant and jobs for the destitute. The jobs should be ones that provide the necessities of life.

"These necessities are food, water, shelter, education, and medical aide. Where there are things that need to be done, but no tokens to pay for the labor, gather those not working and start the project on your own. When others see something being done that will benefit all, they will contribute their help. At the very least, they will provide food and shelter. The people will feel good about their accomplishments and the good things they are bringing about without the Darklord's help. They will find the power of loving one another. They will no longer believe the lies of the Darklord. They will no longer believe that they need him to survive.

"If they stop watching the story boxes and do things with their neighbors and children, they will accomplish so much. In spending time with each other and helping and loving each other, no one will feel isolated and lonely. They won't need the forgetful waters to hide the pain of loneliness and poverty. If they don't drink the forgetful waters, they won't be so cruel to each other and the cycle of pain will stop and their hearts and minds will begin to heal.

"There may not be time for all of this to happen before the judgment falls. There will be many natural disasters, earthquakes, floods, the earth ripping apart, and new mountains rising, volcanoes erupting, and stars falling from the skies. All of this is to try to get the horses to turn from their selfish ways and look to the Father for guidance and to cause them to shed those things that don't matter and cling to those that do. He wants them to realize that things will pass away, but the love they have for each other and the entire world is what is forever. If they can love the Father and each other and share, then they will find their true happiness in each other's joy and victory."

"It is an awesome task. How can we make a difference?"

"One soul at a time. And if that one reaches those around him, then in a shorter time than you think, they can become of one mind and one purpose—to love each other and help each other. The wars will end and peace will reign and joy and harmony abound.

"Will you do this?"

"We will do this!" they cried in unison. And with that they raced towards the Shadowlands, each wondering if it was already too late, but determined to make a difference.

Sara softly closed the book. She and Daniel gazed long and thoughtfully at each other. Time seemed to stand still. Beside them the angel candle flickered and flared. "Mom, can we make a difference?" asked Daniel thoughtfully.

"Yes, Son, I believe we can."

Daniel thought for a minute. "You know, Mom, it will be fun thinking of ways to show the people around us that we care about them. Maybe if they know how good it feels when we do nice things for them, they'll want to do nice things for the people around them."

Sara smiled. Perhaps there was hope of peace on earth after all. She knew that she and Daniel would be doing their part. After all, it only takes a spark to get a fire going. No longer did she feel the deep sadness. Now she felt a sense of purpose and determination rising strong within her heart. Yes, this love was a powerful fire. She felt the chains of dreariness, sadness, and despair melting away. She and Daniel had a mission in life; they would make a difference. With God's help they would claim their town back one person at a time!

Already ideas of how she and Daniel could show their neighbors that they cared about them were tumbling over each other in her mind. The lonely old man downstairs would probably not be so crabby if she were to take him a gift of her homemade bread and jelly and visit with him sometimes. The neighbors that were always screaming at their kids would probably enjoy some time to themselves. Perhaps she and Daniel could take the kids to the park and let them have some fun without the screaming. Yes, each day would be a new adventure to see how much of a difference they could make.

Daniel was thinking too. "Mom, I think sometimes it helps people know we care if we just smile at them and ask how they're doing. Sometimes I could pick some flowers for the old grandma down the hall. Maybe then she'll smile and not screech at us kids for being so noisy."

"I think we're on the right track, Son. With God's help we can show others the way to live. When they see how much we love them, then maybe they'll begin to understand how much God loves them. I think that when they begin to see His love in us that they will want to follow Him, too, and love their neighbors."

That night, Sara and Daniel slept soundly with sweet smiles. Their hearts were soaring on wings of love.

Darby Lynn Gaynor, PO Box 945
Richland, WA 99352
darbygirl99336@charter.net

To order additional copies of

THE LEGEND OF THE SWAN HORSE

Have your credit card ready and call:

1-877-421-READ (7323)

or please visit our web site at
www.pleasantword.com

Also available at:
www.amazon.com
and
www.barnesandnoble.com.

Printed in the United States
18980LVS00002B/118-540